Almost Home

DAUGHTERS OF THE FAITH SERIES

Almost Home

A STORY BASED ON THE LIFE OF
THE *MAYFLOWER'S* MARY CHILTON

Wendy Lawton

MOODY PRESS
CHICAGO

Printed in the United States of America

For my mother, Ruth Johnson Smith,
who not only made a warm and loving earthly home,
but who also guided us toward our spiritual home

Contents

Acknowledgments

Special thanks to Lois Coffey for introducing me to her ancestor Mary Chilton. I owe a debt of gratitude to my brother, James R. Smith, for his hours and hours of library and Internet genealogical work on Mary. And much is owed to Caleb Johnson, owner of the *Mayflower Web Pages* at http://members.aol.com/calebj/mayflower.html, for his tireless devotion to scholarly research and his generosity in sharing that research.

1
Windmills and Wounded Hearts

"Mary!" The shout was punctuated by vigorous pounding on the door.

Mary jumped, poking herself with the sewing needle. She stuck the smarting finger into her mouth to keep the drop of blood from staining the *brocade* sleeve she'd been stitching.

"Coming!"

She managed to slide her needle into the lining fabric for safekeeping.

The yelling and banging on the door grew more insistent. "Mary Chilton!"

Mary opened the heavy wooden door to find the errand lad, Cornelijs.

His breath came in gasps. "Your father was set upon by a pack of boys. They pelted him with rocks. Isabella sent me to fetch you." He pressed his side. "Go quick, Mary. He be bleeding somethin' awful."

Her father? Bleeding? Just a few minutes after Mother

and the girls went to work at the linen mill, James Chilton had left to take a small stack of bodices to Mary's oldest sister, Isabella, for embroidery. Whatever could have happened?

"Where is he, Cornelijs?"

"By the windmill near the Grote School. Close to Bell Alley."

Mary grabbed a jumble of linen strips from the scrap basket and rummaged in the *apothecary chest,* finding a small packet of *sticking plaster.* She shoved them into her apron pocket and poured some water from the tin basin into a clay jug before setting out.

She ran along the canal bank, wishing the April thaw had not come. How much faster it would have been if she could have strapped skates to her shoes and skated along the frozen canal like she and her older sisters, Ingle and Christian, did all winter long. Instead, windmills creaked, and the oars from brightly painted canal boats splashed through the water on this breezy spring morning. Doors on many of the cottages stood open as housewives swept or scrubbed their much-prized blue tile floors.

Mary stopped once, bending over to catch her breath, but she did not tarry long. Why did Isabella have to move all the way over to the other side of the tract when she married Roger?

As Mary neared Bell Alley she saw a cluster of people. She made out Isabella talking and gesturing widely to a constable. Drawing closer, Mary heard her sister's anxious voice.

"My father delivered some of the tailoring work to my home and picked up the lace cuffs I finished." Isabella's words caught in her throat. "When he left, I watched from my doorway as he walked alongside the canal."

Isabella spotted Mary. "Oh, I'm so glad you're here, Mary. Elder Brewster came, but I knew you'd be along. I dare not leave the children, and I did not know . . ."

"Go ahead and help the constable finish," Mary interrupted, moving toward the knot of people. Though Mary was nearly twenty years younger than her sister, they understood each other. Isabella hated the sight of blood.

Still sounding flustered, Isabella turned back to the constable and continued. "My father passed the alley, and a gang of boys came out to taunt him. They said something about English killjoys."

Mary could picture it. That kind of thing happened too often. The tolerant Dutch considered it "merriment" carried a little too far. To the sober English *Separatists* like her family, it felt more like harassment.

William Brewster crouched beside her father. As Mary came near, she cringed. Blood matted Father's gray hair and ran down his face from the jagged gash on his forehead. Mary's lungs stung from running. With the blood, the noise, and the milling people, her knees weakened and started to buckle.

"Do not be alarmed, Mary," said Elder Brewster. "Scalp wounds bleed heavily, but they are usually not as bad as they seem. Once we get him home, we will fetch the surgeon, Jacob Hey, to stitch the wound."

Mary stiffened, shaking off the momentary wooziness. "I brought plaster and bandages."

"Thank you, Daughter," her father said with a wobble in his voice. "I can always trust you to take good care of me." He tried to smile but winced instead.

Mary set to work cleaning the gaping wound with water-soaked linen rags. Father closed his eyes and leaned slightly against his friend as she worked. Mary poured a bit of plaster onto a nearby paving stone and dripped two or three drops of water onto the white powder—just enough to make a sticky paste to cover the open gash and stop the bleeding.

As she worked, Mary listened to Isabella tell the constable how the boys picked up stones when Father ignored their taunts. Though they probably intended only to impress each other with their bravado, one rock hit Father with staggering force. The boys scattered.

Mary clenched her teeth rather than risk saying something harsh. She had seen them before. Those boys paraded around Leyden wearing fancy plumed hats and embroidered *doublets* over puffy-padded short *breeches*. Instead of a collar they sported enormous stiffened *ruffs*. Ribbons and bows encircled their *breeches* and decorated their shoes. They resembled a flock of fancy roosters, strutting to show off colorful plumage.

And, for some reason, nothing infuriated them like the plainly dressed men of the Green Gate congregation.

The constable shook his head as he wrote out Isabella's complaint for the *magistrate*. "These big boys have too much spirit in them, but soon they will take their rightful place at the mill." He paused and nodded. "Aye . . . and then their proud necks will be bent to work."

When she finished tending her father, Mary hugged her sister good-bye. "Hurry back to the children, Isabella. Elder Brewster said he would help me see Father home."

Isabella kissed her father's cheek and hesitantly left to go back to her little ones.

Mary poured the rest of the water over her hands, washing the plaster off her fingers and drying her hands on her apron. She gathered the bundle of lace cuffs from the stones at the edge of the canal. Taking Father's arm, she and Elder Brewster helped him to his feet. His normally white collar was creased and soaked with blood. Why would anyone act so cruelly?

Elder Brewster kept breathing deeply through his nostrils. Mary had known him ever since her family moved to Leyden. She recognized his agitation.

"James, I am fair worried about our children," Elder Brewster said.

Mary's father stiffened. "Surely you do not think those boys would attack the children of our congregation. The *magistrate* was right. They just got carried away. Someone tossed a rock and an insult, and it seemed like sport to them." He stopped to catch his breath as they continued to move slowly along the canal. "The Dutch people have been most hospitable, William."

"That I know, James, but the Dutch folk are too easy on their children. They allow them far too much and require far too little. I worry about the influence on our children."

"Aye," Father said. "The younger children in our congregation prefer speaking Dutch over English, and some of the older ones long for the richly decorated clothing."

Mary wished she could speak up, but she knew no one would appreciate a twelve-year-old girl's thoughts on so weighty a matter. For her, 'twasn't so much wishing for beautiful clothes and the colorful life of the Leyden people; 'twas that she yearned to belong—to really belong.

As they walked along the dike, Mary noticed newly in-habited stork nests atop the roofs on many of the colorful cot-tages. They passed a windmill with flower-filled window boxes on the first floor where the miller's family lived. Slivers of green poked through the soil of a well-tended flower garden —the promise of lilies to come. How Mary loved the beauty and cleanliness of Leyden. One day each week was set aside for scrubbing, and the housewives of Leyden scrubbed every-thing in sight. They hauled buckets of water out of the canals and splashed the water against the houses and onto the street as they mopped and scrubbed and rubbed and polished.

I don't know where I belong, but someday—if it please the Lord—let me have a house to scrub. Someday, let me have a plot of land for planting. And someday let me unpack our linens and smooth out the wrinkles and lay them in a press. Someday ...

As Elder Brewster continued to talk with her father, she silently prayed one final request—*And please, give me room in that someday garden to tuck in a flower or two.* Flowers meant you planned to stay.

❧   ❧   ❧   ❧

Mary remembered very little about moving from Sand-wich in Kent, England, to Holland nearly ten years ago. She was still in *leading strings* when they left, but even now in Leyden, she sometimes dreamed about the smell of salty sea air and the sound of water lapping up against the quay at Sand-wich harbor.

She remembered loving her English house with its white-washed stone walls. When she played outdoors she would sing a bumpity-bump song as she dragged her fingers across the rough surface, getting the chalky white all over her hands.

Another picture Mary could never forget was the disturbing pile of belongings carefully bundled together and secured with twine—as if the Chiltons were preparing to move at a moment's notice.

Her memories got tangled with the stories her sisters told, but early on she learned to watch her parents' faces for signs of worry. Trouble seemed to swirl all around them. Even though she caught only snippets of what was happening, she understood the danger.

"Do you remember why we left England?" Mother had asked one day a few years ago as she, Mary, and Isabella hemmed linens. Isabella's wedding was to take place that August, and they were finishing her *dower chest*.

"Not altogether. I do know that there was trouble and that it had to do with St. Peter's." Mary thought for a minute. "When Isabella or Christian or Ingle took me for a walk, I always wanted to go out near the water so I could go in and out of that mossy stone gate."

"Aye. That was Fishergate. You have such a good memory. You were not quite three," Mother said.

"And did Mary ever get mad when I had to change the route and take the long way around so as not to pass the church," Isabella said with a laugh.

"I did not." It wasn't anger; it was that funny longing she often experienced. She missed walking by St. Peter's, because she used to make-believe that the tower was a medieval castle. It was complicated. She did not miss it because it was where she belonged; she missed it because she never had the chance to belong.

"I shall never forget those last days in England," said Isabella.

"Nor will I," Mother said as she tensed her shoulders over her hemstitching.

Later her mother had told her about the church service at the Hooke home when Andrew Sharpe came into the room to fetch help. Mary's mother, along with Goodwife Hooke and Goodwife Fletcher, left in the middle of the service to assist with the birthing of the Sharpe baby. The poor little babe died, and Mother helped lay the tiny coffin into the ground while the elder said words.

The Chiltons knew their church services were illegal. The Church of England had become little more than another institution of the English government, but it was the only recognized church. Church officials were appointed because of the favors their families performed for British royalty, not because they longed to serve God. Though still called a church, it was not a place where people often met Christ or deepened their faith. Church officials spent more time reading the newly released sonnets of the Stratford-upon-Avon *bard*, William Shakespeare, than they did the Bible—after all, they had met Shakespeare in London.

The Chiltons and many of their friends refused to take part in what they believed were empty rituals, including the meaningless funeral rites. They studied the Bible and wanted to experience a fresh faith and the freedom to worship as they pleased.

The fight was on.

King James believed these *dissenters* were chipping away at the very foundations of England. *Separatists*, like Mary's family, were being imprisoned and persecuted all across England. Some were even hanged for refusing to give up their beliefs. A few slipped out of the country into Holland where freedom of religion existed, but the English authorities watched the ports to keep these troublesome citizens from escaping.

The situation had grown increasingly worse for Mary's family. Church officials paid a visit to the Chilton home. One clergyman spent the entire time yelling and pounding the table till the veins bulged on his neck. They charged her mother with "privately burying a child." According to them, she broke English law and she broke church law.

Mary's father had long been trying to secure passage on a ship out of England, but it was not until the *magistrates* came with an arrest warrant for Mother that the final details hastily fell into place.

Mary could remember bits and pieces of the event. Words swirled around her—words like *excommunication* and prison. And always . . . the soft sobbing of her mother, the worried face of her father, and the bundles of their belongings disappearing one at a time as Father secretly stowed them aboard a ship waiting in the harbor.

꿍   꿍   꿍   꿍

The last time Mary saw her English home she stood tiptoe on a wooden crate so she could peer over the salty-tasting rail. The ship carrying the Chiltons and all their belongings left the mouth of the River Stour into the Strait of Dover and headed toward the North Sea and Holland. The stone walls and arched bridges guarding the town of Sandwich eventually faded into the shimmer of water as the flap, flap, flap of sails being unfurled signaled that she was headed into the unknown.

❦   ❦   ❦   ❦

"Mary, are you growing weary?" Elder Brewster's concern drew Mary back to the conversation between her father and Elder Brewster. As usual she had been daydreaming.

"No, Elder," she replied.

Elder Brewster took Mary at her word. He turned back to his friend. "The Dutch people have been kind," said the elder. "I'll not be finding fault with them."

"I know," her father said. "Since coming from England it is so difficult to make a living. Leyden is mostly a good, wholesome place, but it holds little promise for us. We work in the linen mills or the woolen factories, and our wives must work and our children work, and yet . . . we have nothing."

"Aye," said Elder Brewster. "When some of our brothers think back to their land holdings in England, it becomes easy to get discouraged. We need to remember the terrible persecution back in England. Here, at least, we worship as we choose."

"But I long to own land again," her father said as he wiped aside a piece of sticky blood-matted hair. "Sometimes I look out onto those fields where the drying linen stretches out for miles and miles and I . . ."

Mary knew her father would not finish. He could not put that ache into words, but she often watched the longing in his face as he looked onto the bleaching fields near their home.

He would squint his eyes, and she guessed that he pictured fields of grain like he used to have at home.

But her father always changed the subject away from the sentimental. "It worries me, William, that the English authorities plot to have you returned to England." Elder Brewster was only a few years younger than her father, but James Chilton took a fatherly interest in all members of the congregation. "You be careful, William Brewster, with that little printing press of yours."

"Aye. Our *Choir Alley Press* is beginning to rattle a few windows in Merrie Old England." That was an understatement. The press, sometimes called the *Pilgrim Press,* secretly published several books that infuriated King James and his bishops. Elder Brewster abruptly changed the subject. "So, you are planning on making the move with us then, James?"

Move? Mary dropped her father's arm. "Move, Father?" Surely she heard wrong. She'd seen no bundles piling up in the hall. "What do you mean, Elder Brewster?"

The elder spoke in a soft voice, "Mary, take your father's arm. I did not mean to speak out of turn."

Mary lifted her father's arm again, and, as he seemed to slump against her, she whispered, "We are almost home, Father." Elder Brewster's question still rang in her ears, as she repeated the soothing words, "Almost home."

A deep ache began to grow in Mary's chest, and no matter how quickly she blinked her eyes, she felt the sting of threatening tears.

2
Farewell to Leyden

"Mary, your father left for Isabella's to finish the last of the *breeches* for *Mynheer* van Blitterswijck. Ingle and Christian hastened to the weavers for cloth. We still have much work to be completed." Mary's mother paused in her sorting and bundling of *doublet* pieces.

Mary sensed there was more, but she waited for her mother to go on. From the sound of Mother's lighthearted movement this morning, it was bound to be good.

"Mistress Tilley invited you to come to their house. She said that Elizabeth could help you *baste* these *interfacings* so that they'll be ready for Father to tailor. Mistress Brewster said that Fear can come as well."

The spring day had already dawned fair, but to Mary it got even brighter. A whole morning spent with her friends Fear and Elizabeth. "Thank you, Mother. We shall work hard."

Mother smiled. "How I wish you did not have to work so

hard, but even with all of us working we barely put aside anything." She looked toward the open top half of the door, but her eyes did not seem to focus on anything in particular. "If only . . ." Her words drifted off.

"Oh, Mother, I'm happy to help. And when my friends sew with me, 'tis ever so much more fun."

Mother now stayed home to help with the tailoring—no more going off to the mill each morning. With all of them working—Isabella at her house and Mary and her sisters at home—they were able to satisfy Father's tailoring customers much sooner.

'Twas not the only change. So much had happened in the year since the rock-throwing incident. Though talk continued off and on about an eventual move, no immediate plans developed. Some in the congregation talked of going to the Virginia colony, but the news coming back from America sounded grim. The rumors included deaths, savages, and starvation. Others in the congregation read of Sir Walter Raleigh's lush tropical Guiana and wanted to settle there. Mary tried to ignore the talk that circled around their Green Gate congregation.

Elder Brewster had sailed for London a year earlier on business for the congregation. Nearly every morning Father met with Pastor Robinson, Deacon Carver, and the other men to pray for the elder's safety. The English searched continuously for Elder Brewster. Some of the congregation's Dutch friends told them to keep a watch out for English officials secretly sent into Holland to find him, but so far God kept Elder Brewster safe. Now he traveled right under English noses.

No real future existed for the Pilgrims in Leyden. Mary knew that, but she savored her time in Holland. If she could just freeze the rush of time as winter freezes the flow in the canal, she could be happy. As long as Mother did not start bundling their belongings, Mary was content. Bundles piling up in the hall always signaled that change was in the air.

"Mary, come help me sort and stack, so you can be on your way," Mother said.

"Sorry, Mother."

"Woolgathering again?" When Mother smiled, her eyes seemed to crinkle into their own merry smiles. "I'm half afraid to mention that Mistress Tilley invited the three of you to stay for dinner and then work the afternoon as well."

Mary pressed her lips together for fear that no sensible word could possibly form on her lips. She longed to run and jump for the sheer joy of it, but a girl of thirteen no longer hopped around like a child.

Mother packed the market basket with work while Mary pulled her shawl around her shoulders and pinned it. She started to curtsey her good-bye to Mother, but reached out and hugged her instead. Swinging the basket, Mary headed along the canal toward the Hopkins's home.

She couldn't help the bounce in her step. The sunshine falling on her face felt warm for spring. She smiled at everyone she met along the way, even the workmen unloading sheaves of thatch from a cart.

Mary hummed the melody of the *Old One-Hundredth*. Before long the words began to form, just as she had learned them from the *Ainsworth Psalter*.

Shout to Jehovah, all the earth;
Serve ye Jehovah with gladness
Before Him come with singing mirth;
Know that Jehovah He God is

She rounded the corner toward Green Gate and hurried to join Fear Brewster at the door of the Tilley cottage. Elizabeth opened the door before they knocked. Mistress Tilley stood behind her.

"Welcome, friends," said Elizabeth, sounding grown-up. "Come in."

Elizabeth's mother laughed. "Elizabeth wants to play the perfect hostess, but I keep telling her 'tis a work party not a merriment." Mistress Tilley straightened Elizabeth's cap to cover more of the girl's soft brown hair.

"It's merry enough for me," said Mary. "Thank you for inviting us. Having a whole day to visit will be like the old times when we could play for hours and hours without a care." Mary stepped inside and felt the warmth of the banked fire.

"I do not remember feeling carefree," said Fear. "I used to worry that Elizabeth would fall in the canal." Fear's eyes always widened when she recalled some of Elizabeth's hair-raising antics.

"That's why they named you Fear." Elizabeth teased Fear about her name, but they all knew it stood for Fear of God. Her parents chose descriptive names—like her younger brother's name, Love. It was short for Love of God. Her littlest brother was Wrestling, taken from Wrestling with the Devil. Their names afforded them no end of teasing.

"'Tis a wonder I did not push you headlong into the canal, Elizabeth," Fear said.

"Before you two start a brawl, shall I divide up the work?" Mary placed her workbasket on the table.

Each girl claimed her favorite spot on the benches at the table. Mary put the basket of work beside her and handed pieces of corded silk and woolen *interfacing* to her friends. Fear took her *needle case, pin poppet,* and *thimble case* out of her embroidered *sweetbag.* The other two settled in and did the same. Their sewing tools numbered among their most prized possessions. Needles and pins were especially *dear.* As the girls talked, they threaded needles and took felted pieces of wool and began to *baste* the felt to the silk outer fabric. Mary showed them how to curve and shape the fabric as they laid in the stitches. They talked and stitched, bending the cloth over their hands just where the curve of a shoulder would come and laying in *basting* stitches to hold the shape.

"Mother decided to cook hodgepodge for dinner," Elizabeth announced. "And a boiled pudding."

"Mmmmm." Mary loved the taste of savory Dutch hodgepodge stew, and nothing was quite as good as a boiled pudding served with butter.

"Father keeps wishing for Indian corn to add to the stew," Elizabeth said. "When Father's cousin sailed to Jamestown Colony and back, he brought corn."

"Indian corn? I thought he starved while he lived in America," Fear said, looking up from her sewing.

"He didn't starve all the time." Elizabeth always managed to bring up their cousin's travels in America. Very few in their congregation had traveled far, let alone to the struggling Jamestown Colony.

"Please, let us not talk about faraway places." Mary wished they could stay in the Tilleys' hall forever. "Maybe the Lord kept your cousin safe so he could come home to his family and so he could tell our congregation about the dangers abroad."

"But he does not fear the dangers, Mary." As Elizabeth shook her head, a strand of her hair loosened from under her *coif*. "He yearns for the rich land of America." She finished a side panel and reached for another.

Mary frowned, stabbing her needle into the fabric with an audible clink as it jammed against her thimble.

Elizabeth tilted her head as if she did not understand. "Mary, surely you know that Elder Brewster and Deacon Cushman already received our *patent* to journey to Virginia." She paused, looking hard at Mary. "All that remains is to buy a ship and arrange for provisions."

Fear spoke gently, "I thought you knew, Mary. The men talk about it at every gathering."

Mary smoothed her work and wove the needle into the lining for safekeeping. Placing her piece in the workbasket, she stood up without responding and politely excused herself. Let her friends assume she went outside to the *privy*. Mary could not bear to sit a moment longer. Her stomach felt hollow. *Leaving Holland? Could this be true? Maybe our family will not be going—after all, Father is sixty-three years old. He is the oldest man in the congregation.*

And what about my sisters? Isabella has two little children— she just started her life. Surely she will stay in Holland. Ingle's

Robert lives in Leyden, as does Christian's beau. Would they leave?

The once-sunny day dimmed. As Mary walked between the canal and the Hopkins's cottage, she ran hands along the brick wall—humming a sad bumpity-bumpity song from days long gone.

Am I the only one to feel like a dandelion puff about to be blown to the wind? Mary looked up in time to see a stork flying to the nest above the roof. A verse she had once memorized from Scripture came suddenly to mind: *The foxes have holes, and the birds of the air have nests; but the Son of man hath not where to lay his head.*

So I'm not the only one to feel this way, thought Mary, as she walked back into the hall filled with savory smells and quiet conversation. It helped to remember that her Lord knew.

Her friends were right. Three months later Mary sorted through belongings with her mother and sisters, bundling the essentials and stacking them in the passageway. The Chiltons had decided to join the first wave of Pilgrims traveling to the New World.

Not all the Chiltons, thought Mary. *How will I ever say farewell to Isabella?* Her oldest sister yearned to come, but her children were still so little. Roger told her they would join the congregation in America later. Each time Mary saw Isabella, they reminded each other that someday they would be together again. It did not help stem the sadness.

Even worse, Ingle and Christian had decided to stay in

Holland. Mary refused to even think about the days ahead of them. The few times she contemplated the farewells with her sisters, her chest tightened till she could barely draw breath. She wondered if a heart could really break; hers felt as if a cruel hand encircled it, ever squeezing, tighter and tighter.

Yesterday the congregation had called a day of Solemn Humiliation. That meant that the entire day was spent in deep prayer or, as Pastor Robinson instructed, a time for "pouring out prayers to the Lord with great fervency mixed with an abundance of tears."

Mary contributed plenty to the abundance of tears. During a break in the service, Mary and her friends walked along Stink Alley together—trying to keep from declaring everything a "one last time" event.

Elizabeth walked ahead. Mary held Fear's hand.

"How shall we live without you, Fear?" Mary couldn't bear that Fear must stay behind to help care for those of the Brewster family left in Holland.

"We've talked long and we've talked hard. We cannot all go. We truly do not have the funds." Fear sighed deeply and spoke slowly, as if she were explaining it to a child.

Mary knew that Fear had explained it too many times already. "I know," Mary said, squeezing her friend's hand. "But it does not make it easier, does it?"

The Green Gate congregation had hard decisions to make. Pastor Robinson declared that if more than half the congregation decided to go to America, he would go with them. If less than half went, Elder Brewster would accompany them. As the numbers were tallied, Pastor Robinson was to remain in Holland.

"The worst part," Fear said, "is that I cannot bid farewell to my father." Elder Brewster hid in England—he was still a wanted man. He planned to find a way to slip aboard the ship while docked in England.

"Tell me what you wish to say to him, and I promise I shall deliver your exact words."

Fear said nothing for several minutes. "I want to ponder this, Mary. I wish to find the perfect words. Thank you for your offer."

Fear and Mary caught up with Elizabeth and headed back toward the Meeting House. As they entered, they heard the swell of mournful singing from the pages of the Psalter.

Pastor Robinson opened the Bible to Ezra 8:21 and read, "Then I proclaimed a fast there, at the river of Ahava, that we might afflict ourselves before our God, to seek of him a right way for us, and for our little ones, and for all our substance."

Mary stepped out of the canal boat onto the landing berth at Delft Haven. Leyden lay far behind. Father hoisted bundle after bundle, containing all their worldly possessions, onto a *dray* headed to the ship waiting in the Delft harbor.

A row of canal boats floated on the River Maas, anchored alongside Mary's. The whole Leyden congregation came to see the Pilgrims off. Mary could not bear to look at faces. She reached down and scooped up a handful of soil. *Truth be told, I never belonged to Holland, but Holland worked its way into my heart.*

She could not bring herself to cast the soil down, so she

wrapped it in her hankie and tucked it deep into her leather pouch.

Pastor Robinson fell to his knees, and everyone did the same as he committed the little band of Pilgrims to the Lord. As the prayers ended, the group silently looked 'round the circle. Mary tried to memorize each face. She could not help but wonder if this would be their last time together this side of eternity.

Mistress Brewster stood with her two young boys, Love and Wrestling. Tears streamed down her face as she kissed her three older children good-bye.

Mary could put it off no longer. Her sisters had already bid wrenching farewells to their parents. Mary hugged Isabella and Roger and the babies. "Next year, Isabella," Mary insisted. "Next year you will come to America."

"Aye, Little Sister. Aye." Isabella could say no more. As she pulled away, she pressed a twine-wrapped bundle into Mary's hands. "For America, Mary."

"Write letters to us if you can," Mary said to Ingle and Christian. "We must not lose each other. I will watch for each ship, praying that it brings word from you."

Mary watched her sisters huddle together. Over the last few weeks they had all talked about being brave, but now that the time for parting had come, the Chiltons wept openly.

As Mary and her parents began to move toward the *Speedwell* docked at the *quay,* Fear rushed up to embrace her friend. "Tell my father that I love him," she whispered, "and that I will care for things in Holland. Tell him that I will walk with the Lord, and I will come to America as soon as he sends for me."

"I will tell him those things," Mary said. "I promise."

As she picked up a bundle and headed toward the *quay*, Mary prayed, "Keep them safe, Father. And keep us safe as well."

Later, as the *Speedwell* headed out toward the North Sea, Mary took one last look at the beautiful Delft Haven and added another short prayer. "And, Lord, let me find a place to belong—to really belong."

3

Trouble on the Open Seas

The *Speedwell* covered the distance from Holland to England in good time, but her tendency to *list* and tip offered the passengers a drenching with every roll. Mary and Elizabeth thought it great sport at first, but when their clothing grew stiff from the salt and their petticoats dragged water with every step, they longed for dry land.

The leakiness didn't make sense. When the Pilgrims bought the ship, they had completely refitted her—everything was new. Once settled in their new land, the *Speedwell* was to sail between America and England. The larger ship, the *Mayflower*, waited for them in Southampton, but she was only a chartered vessel for one passage. When she safely delivered her passengers and cargo to the New World, she would head back to England. 'Twas the *Speedwell*, their own ship, that would carry the Pilgrims' salted fish, lumber, and valuable pelts back to England and return supplies, mail, and passengers from England to the New World.

By the time the *Speedwell* rounded the chalk cliffs of
Dover, however, concern among the crew and passengers
grew. The ship leaked like a worn-out pudding bag. The
sailors checked for holes but found none. Mary kept hearing
the words "general weakness." It sounded alarming.

"Father," Mary asked, "do you think the whole trip to
America will be this wet?" Her ginger-colored hair usually
sprung tiny corkscrews of curls out from under her *coif*, leaving her to forever poke them back under. Instead, strings of
sopping hair lay darkly plastered to her neck. She shivered
with cold.

"Once we land at Southampton, we'll undertake repairs
yet again," Father said. "Her rig remains faulty, though it was
replaced before the last voyage to Holland. And we fear the
new mast is too heavy for her and she carries too much sail."

"Isn't that costly?" Mary knew they had little extra money.

"Aye." Father sighed. "And even more worrisome is that
our departure will be delayed."

Even though the news troubled her, Mary was glad her
father spoke frankly. She understood that the later the departure, the colder and more treacherous the ocean journey
would become. Arriving in America just as the winter settled
on the land was even more dangerous. There would be precious little time to build shelter and no chance of growing
food to get them through the winter.

As Mary stood pondering their troubles, she looked at the
bundles of their belongings banked against the sea chest. On
top of the pile was the gift Isabella gave her in Delft. At the
time Isabella had pressed it into her hands, Mary had decided
to wait till she landed in America to open it. It linked her to

home and family. Besides, from the time she was little, Mary loved looking forward to a surprise. Before the water drenched everything, Mary tied a scrap of oilcloth around it to make sure it stayed dry.

When the *Speedwell* finally sloshed into Southampton, Mary and Elizabeth were relieved to wring themselves out and step onto dry land. Once on England's shores again, the small band of Pilgrims tried to stay out of sight as much as possible, boarding with other *Separatists* until time to embark for America.

The two friends spent much of their time watching the repairs to the *Speedwell*. They remained careful not to attract notice. Anti-*Separatist* sentiment still ran deep, and the girls knew better than to risk inflaming those feelings.

The *Mayflower* stood at anchor nearby. The brightly painted ship had a jutting beak, much like a seabird, and a high, elegant aftercastle. She was compact, but Mary liked the way she rode in the water. She had heard the sailors talking, and she now knew that the *Mayflower* was a 180-ton *bark-rigged* merchant ship. Mary even knew that the ship carried 525 square yards of canvas. When 'twas time to finally set sail, Mary happily discovered that her family had been assigned to the *Mayflower*.

"We sail on the *Mayflower* as well." Elizabeth managed a wide smile as she struggled under bundles of supplies to be loaded onboard.

"What an adventure we shall have," Mary said as she helped Elizabeth hoist the bundles into the longboat that would have to row them out to the *Mayflower* moored in the harbor. In spite of missing her sisters and Holland, and in spite of worrying about the ordeal ahead, Mary anticipated the bustle and tension of the adventure.

On board the ship, the Pilgrims spent a busy few days stringing canvas across the main deck for a little privacy. They arranged their goods and tried to get used to their cramped spaces. The sailors and cargo handlers packed the hold with food and supplies. Many of the Pilgrims' stores for the New World—like seeds and implements and even livestock—were crammed in alongside the ship's cargo.

Mary managed to squeeze down into the hold to take a look at it all. It seemed like such plenty—barrel after barrel of ale and water, more barrels of hardtack biscuit and flour, cases of dried meat, and even baskets of vegetables.

The Pilgrims also met the other passengers who joined the company in England. The Green Gate congregation's small hoard of money had dwindled fast as they purchased supplies, bought and refurbished the *Speedwell,* and chartered the *Mayflower.* Financial investors offered to give them the money needed for their costly venture. In exchange, the Pilgrims signed an agreement that they would pay the businessmen— mainly with fish, lumber, and furs—within seven years.

The investors determined to fill the ships with passengers, so they also recruited people from England. These families sought a better life than England offered. They never even considered religious freedom in making their decision to travel to America. Before too long, the two groups of Pilgrims came to know each other, but Mary always heard the Leyden group referred to as the Saints, and the English group as the Strangers.

Even before they set sail, Elizabeth and Mary met one

Stranger who became a friend almost immediately. Constance Hopkins and her family joined the Pilgrims at Southampton, but their family didn't believe in strangers—they considered every person their friend or else their soon-to-be friend. Constance was but a few months older than Elizabeth and Mary, yet she laughed, teased, and made everything seem like fun— even lugging their things aboard ship.

At long last they settled in. The ship's master, Captain Christopher Jones, grudgingly gave the Leyden congregation leave to pray for just a moment, then he nodded his head at the *bosun* and the adventure began.

The *bosun* sang out the orders, and the sailors moved with precision as they climbed the rigging to loose the sheets and unfurl the sails. With a loud flap-slap-slap sound the canvas filled with wind, and the stiff breeze carried the little ship out to sea.

Mary leaned over the rail to watch the froth whipped up by the bow cutting through the waves. The ship pitched, but not as badly as the *Speedwell* had on the voyage from Holland to England. Mary worried as she looked over to see the *Speedwell*'s strange limping gait. The newly repaired ship pitched and then rolled from side to side. *Why would the* Speedwell *lurch like that when the Mayflower leapt gracefully through the waves?*

Constance crept up behind Mary and put her hands over Mary's eyes. "Guess who?" she sang out.

"Hmmm. Perchance 'tis the only person I know who still plays nursery games." Mary could tell from the giggles that both Constance and Elizabeth had joined her on deck.

"Thou art no fun. Truth be told, thou art an old stick."

Constance poked fun at the way many of the Pilgrims talked. She removed her hands and gave Mary an excited hug. "Dost thou think thou shouldst put on a hat, Maid Mary? Any more freckles on that fair face of thine and wilt rival John Goodman's spaniel."

"Constance!" Elizabeth burst into laughter. "You told me you admire Mary's freckles and ginger-colored hair."

"Aye, Mistress Constance. You but wish you were dappled as nicely as me," teased Mary as she pinched her new friend.

The movement of the ship, the singsong orders shouted to the sailors, and the frenzied cry of seabirds added to their exuberance.

"Just think," said Elizabeth in a mock-serious voice. "It's a beautiful August morning in the year of our Lord 1620 . . ."

"Oh fiddle," interrupted Constance. "Now who sets about to be big, Deacon Elizabeth?"

The morning was too fair to tussle, and the friends ended up in a gale of giggles. Most of the Pilgrims climbed below deck as soon as the Southampton shore disappeared into the morning sun. Mary knew the English farewells were hard on those who left family and friends on shore. There had been tears enough in Delft for Mary. Her heart was just scabbing over. She *lief* not poke at the raw wound. Better to trade joy for tears, even if one had to work at it. She may have had to say farewell to her grown sisters, but she still had Mother and Father. Even if you didn't belong to a place, you belonged to your parents.

Turning their backs toward the bow, the three girls took the wind full in the face. It knocked their *coifs* right off their heads, and, like the whipping of the ship's sails, the linen caps flapped against their necks, held only by the tie at the back of their necks.

Mary's friends pulled up their *coifs* and turned toward the bow. Not Mary; she took hers off. The wind full on her face, the spray of the sea misting around her, and the rhythmic slicing of the ocean exhilarated her. Strands of hair whipped across her cheeks, catching in her mouth, but she didn't care. *Please, Almighty Father,* she prayed silently, *let this be my journey home.* That word *home* rang in her heart. Perchance this journey would carry the Chiltons out of trouble and finally give them a safe home. The shrieking gulls, the snapping ropes, and the percussion of the sails seemed to say, "Mary, you are almost home."

"You!" It was the furious voice of a sailor. "Aye, I'm talking to you, ye little puke-stockings."

Mary looked up in the rigging to see who hurled angry words. The sailor had a foothold in the rigging and an arm wrapped around the *mizzenmast* as he leaned out and yelled across the length of the ship at them.

Elizabeth shrank in toward Mary, "Is he talking to us?"

"Aye," said Constance. "Let us go down below before he becomes profane."

As Mary opened the hatch and grabbed the ladder, she heard him laugh a swaggering bellow of a laugh.

"Ho! That took the wind out of their prissy little sails," he boasted to the sailors on the decks.

"Aye, Stubbs. Now to make sure them puke-stockings keep their brats locked in the 'tween decks," another said.

Father frowned as the girls settled in between a sea chest

and a crate. He must have overheard the taunt. Mary and her friends no longer felt like talking much. The sailors disliked the Pilgrims on sight. If their torment kept up, chances were it would be a long journey.

"When Elder Brewster . . . er . . . when he comes aboard, we will speak to Master Jones about the actions of his crew."

"Elder Brewster? Aboard?" Mary looked at her father, who suddenly seemed to be busy with something. *How did someone board a ship once you were already at sea?*

"Mary . . . nay!" Father whispered. He raised his head to look her directly in the eye. Mary recognized the quirk of his eyebrow.

She understood what that "nay" meant. It meant "No questions asked"; it meant "bide your time"; it even meant "hide any curiosity." Mary had not lived a life of danger without learning how to read unspoken warnings. And this was definitely a warning.

Mary could not believe she had forgotten Elder Brewster and her friend Fear—even for a time. *I'm sorry, Fear,* she thought. *Will I ever be able to get your message to your father?*

Constance and Elizabeth had been talking together and missed the conversation with her father, but Mary could not stop thinking about it. In the excitement of leaving, she had not remembered that Elder Brewster planned to slip on board when the officials turned their backs.

But the officials watched the ship and the docks like vultures. They boarded several times before the ship cast off, demanding that Master Jones open the passenger log. One time they even questioned Mistress Brewster.

Mary watched the scene with frustration. They so frightened Mistress Brewster that she could not utter a single word. At their badgering questions, her eyes widened, and she could only shake her head back and forth. The boys, Love and Wrestling, hung on her, one on each leg. Mary noticed that Love started to say something and instead, burst into howls. At the time, Mary thought he was as anxious as his mother was.

Now she was not so sure. She remembered Master Martin, the ship's governor, making a joke later about a "pinch, well placed." Did someone pinch Love? Why would someone pinch him? What was going on?

Constance stood up. "I must help Mother with Damaris," she said, stretching. "Mother has yet to figure out how to prepare a meal using the *brazier*. Besides, I worry that the motion of the ship may leave her queasy."

Constance had confided to Mary and Elizabeth that her real mother died many years ago. Mistress Hopkins was her stepmother and Damaris her half-sister. In their family they worked hard at accepting one another. Constance said it felt better to just call her "Mother" and leave the "step" off.

"Is your mother tired?" asked Elizabeth. Mistress Hopkins's pregnancy was far advanced. She could end up giving birth at sea.

"Aye," said Constance. "Father had hoped for a timely departure. He wanted to be safely installed in America before the birth of the baby, but . . ." She tried to shrug her shoulders, but she hunched them instead and her teeth clenched, making her jaw look tight.

"If you plan to *mind* Damaris," Mary said, "shall I offer to care for Remember and Mary Allerton?" Mistress Allerton's baby would probably come somewhere near the time of Mrs. Hopkins's *confinement*.

"Perchance I should offer to amuse Resolved for Mistress White. She must be just as tired," Elizabeth said.

There could be three births in the cramped quarters of the *Mayflower*. Mary prayed that God would grant them well.

"That's what we can do, then," Mary said, jumping up and pushing the mystery of Elder Brewster out of her mind for now. "We'll be the *Mayflower* nannies, *minding* the little ones for their mothers."

The small group of Pilgrims settled into their temporary home on board the *Mayflower*. The mothers learned to prepare meals on tiny coal *braziers* when the sea was calm, and they learned to serve cold meals when the ocean got choppy and it became too dangerous to have a fire.

The men managed the foodstuffs and supplies. The scarcity of funds for buying provisions in England meant that they needed to ration the supplies. They might very well run short of food and drink for the journey. Much prayer took place over the stores in the hold—prayers for daily bread and prayers that God would somehow multiply their meager rations.

The big boys worked with the men. With the work in the hold finished, they would all go topside to practice their skill with firearms. The man hired to provide their military defense, Captain Myles Standish, grew increasingly worried about their lack of skill and set about drilling them hour after hour. At first some of the travelers balked, but even those first days were long, and the drills provided something to do.

They'd only been to sea a day or two when Mary heard the ropes creak that tethered the longboat to the deck. Why would they be lowering the longboat into the ocean?

"The *Speedwell* is sinkin'!" The rough London boy, John Billington, came thudding down the ladder, shouting the news.

"John, hold your tongue," Master Martin said. His face turned a pasty white, and he followed the men up the ladder.

All conversation hushed below deck until all you heard was the slap of the water against the side of the ship and the gentle creaking of the timbers. Mary thought about their friends aboard the *Speedwell,* such as Master Cushman. *Father, keep them safe.* She remembered the drenching wet of the *Speedwell* and felt guilty that they had been enjoying the more comfortable *Mayflower.*

The sounds topside grew more frenzied—orders yelled from the *bosun* to the crew, sails being furled, footsteps slamming across the deck. After what seemed like hours, Mary felt a funny movement. A barrel tipped over and rolled across the deck.

'Tis turning around. I can feel it—the ship is turning around. She looked at the silent women huddled in their family groups, and she saw the same stricken look mirrored on each face.

4

From Land to Sea
and Back Again

After just a few days at sea, the discouraged band of Pilgrims turned back toward England. The *Speedwell* leaked like a sieve, and, truth be told, they worried 'twas not seaworthy enough to make it back to shore. The ship limped into the port of Dartmouth with the *Mayflower* running escort.

Most of the Leyden congregation waited aboard the *Mayflower,* praying and singing psalms as they battled anxiety and worry. They trusted God to care for them, but as the days ticked away and the repairs on the weakened *Speedwell* dragged on, faces got longer and longer. The cost of repairs on the ship mounted as well.

Mary kept hearing the word "winter" in every conversation.

"We're bound to run into winter storms at sea."

"When we land in America, winter will be in full force, and we'll have no shelter."

"If we arrive mid-winter, how will we plant? We'll have to wait almost three seasons to harvest food."

The worried whispers continued to grow as the days ticked by. After a *fortnight*, they were talking about abandoning the journey. The men gathered in little groups, but privacy was not to be found. The conversations continued both above deck and below as the ship rocked and the gulls screamed and the sailors grumbled.

"But we cannot abandon the journey now. If we use up the stores of food and provisions needed to keep us until spring, however will we replace them?" asked Master Hopkins.

"How indeed," Deacon Carver said. "We must go, and we must trust our fate into the hands of God." Deacon Carver spoke the words, but it was the conviction of every man. You could see it in the set of their jaws. Mary knew then that the adventure would continue.

When the ships finally set sail weeks later on the morning tide, frustration and anxiety had replaced the jubilation of the first departure. To Mary, it seemed as if both ships groaned and creaked their way out of the English Channel toward the open sea.

"At last!" Mary said to Constance and Elizabeth. "I am fair weary with waiting."

"I started wondering if we should ever get off this ship," said Constance.

"And I, as well," said Elizabeth.

Waiting was always hard, but this setback wore them down. The girls stood firmly planted at the rail for this departure, no matter what the sailors might say. In the weeks since their first departure, they had observed that the crew heartily disliked them, and nothing the Pilgrims did seemed to matter.

'Twas like the reaction of the rock-throwing boys in Leyden. The Pilgrims' very presence inflamed the sailors' anger.

When they had been at sea just over a day, the winds picked up, and the girls' spirits lifted ever so slightly. Once again the girls had come topside. Constance bounced Damaris on her hip as she stood at the rail and looked toward the west and America. Mary stood at her side enjoying the prosperous breeze. Elizabeth leaned back against a huge coil of rope and looked past them as she watched the foamy wake left by the ship.

"No!" Elizabeth screamed, as she shook her head in disbelief.

"Elizabeth?" Mary had looked up in time to see Elizabeth's eyes widen and her face drain of all color.

"Mary, Constance . . . look!" Elizabeth pointed toward the *Speedwell.*

They turned around in time to see the *Speedwell heel* so far over that the people on deck grabbed ropes and railings to keep from being washed overboard.

The *bosun* of the *Mayflower* blew the ship's whistle and, without consultation, furled the sails and headed back to England for the second time, running escort for the fatally flawed *Speedwell.*

The *Mayflower* departed from Plymouth, England, by herself this time. 'Twas mid-September—far too late to be starting across the Atlantic Ocean, though the Pilgrims pushed on in spite of the delays. The *Speedwell* and some twenty people stayed behind. The rest jammed into the main cabin on the *Mayflower*. Whatever provisions could be squeezed into the hold had been loaded.

Crossing the ocean unaccompanied would mean certain tragedy if anything should happen to the *Mayflower*, but the Pilgrims trusted God to see them across. Even more worrisome to Mary was that once the *Mayflower* delivered them, they were on their own in a foreign land until friends in England and Holland could charter another ship.

The *Mayflower* had been at sea for several days—long enough that the passengers settled into a routine to pass the time.

Mother sat on the folded featherbed with Mary as she read aloud from *Foxe's Book of Martyrs*. Mother felt it important to continue Mary's studies, even if she couldn't go to school.

Mary set the book down. "Mother, do you miss the girls?"

"Oh, aye, Mary." Mother reached out and, tucking a stray curl under Mary's cap, brushed her hand across Mary's cheek. "I know they are safe, and I know they remain with our congregation, but how I miss them."

"I miss wee Sarah and Samuel too." Mary loved Isabella's children. "Do you think they will remember us?"

"Their own memory may fade, but Isabella will tell them about us. When they come to America, they will recite everything about you from the color of your soft brown eyes to the way you grabbed their arms and swung them 'round in a circle."

Mary smiled at the memory. Even though Samuel wobbled from dizziness when they stopped, he always begged for more.

Mother leaned back against the sea chest. "God weaves families together. 'Tis much like the cloth we weave. When we've filled the whole warp, we must remove the cloth from the loom, even though it settled there so tidily. We cut the weaving, and the pieces go for many different things and to many different places. One lot of cloth may go for waistcoats. Even if those waistcoats end up far and wide, you can always tell that they were cut from the same cloth. If the cloth merely stayed on the loom, how would it fulfill its purpose?"

"But 'tis such a hardship to be torn apart."

"Aye." Mother sat quietly, rocking with the movement of the ship. "I remember when my own mother died. 'Twas as if the center of our family had been ripped out and all the threads around the hole unraveled."

Mary leaned in closer.

"'Twas not easy to find my way after that." Her mother spoke softly, even though no one could overhear in the noisy cabin.

"Did meeting Father help you get better?" Mary did not know how to say it, but she watched the closeness of Father and Mother, and she saw how they helped each other weather hard times.

"No. Your father came long after." Her mother turned toward Mary. "'Tis hard to explain. We say the words 'cast your cares on the Lord' so often that we forget to hear the truth in them. But, during that sad time, 'tis what saved me. I learned to take my aching loneliness and my despair to God."

"And that made it better?"

"Not that easily." Her mother gave a small laugh. "No, Mary, 'twas not that easy—it started out more like wailing at

God, 'Why did you take my mother?' My hurt was so raw that I shrieked like a little child."

Mary hated to think of her mother's loneliness.

"Before long, I noticed that when I cried out, God comforted me." Her mother laughed. "Once I quieted enough to listen, that is. That began my friendship with God. The more I needed Him, the closer He came . . . 'Tis hard to explain."

"I understand a little of it," Mary said, pausing to let the ideas settle.

"Are you going to read further?" Mother asked.

"I need to go for a walk." The tight space and the close smells often sent Mary scrambling up the ladder toward blue sky. "Where is Father? I don't hear any firearm practice."

"He's down talking to Elder Brew— I mean he's down in the hold with the men."

Mother stood up as if to change the subject. She took the tiny straw broom and whisked the floor around the feather bed. As she got on her knees to wipe out the *brazier*, Mary stopped her with a whisper.

"You can tell me, Mother. I think I know what you set about to say."

"Nay, child. Until we are well out at sea, there is too much at stake. You must keep your counsel."

Mary knew that meant she could tell no one. She looked over to the other side of the quarters, and she saw that Constance still played with Damaris while Mistress Hopkins rested. Constance did not even know about Elder Brewster, since she came with the English Pilgrims.

Elizabeth lay next to her tiny cousin, Humility, as the baby napped. The gentle rocking of the ship helped the little ones at naptime. Mary wondered if Elizabeth thought about their friend Fear as much as Mary did. Mary needed to deliver Fear's message to her father.

And now Mary knew Elder Brewster hid in some cranny on this ship. Surely Mistress Brewster would take supper to him, would she not?

Mary watched Mistress Brewster and the boys all that afternoon. She could not keep herself from thinking about Elder Brewster, hidden away on the ship with half his family left behind in Holland and the other half so close he could probably hear their footsteps. Mary understood the ache of having your family scattered to the wind, but to be all alone, with no one . . .

Fear's words would surely comfort her father. And during his time of enforced solitude and hiding, his daughter's message would mean even more.

Mary could relay Fear's words to Mistress Brewster and ask her to pass them on to Elder Brewster. But the message meant so much to Fear. She chose Mary to deliver it to her father. Passing off the message to someone else, even Fear's mother, seemed careless.

When Mistress Brewster finished kneading bread, she slipped out of the cabin. Mary trailed at a distance. Just as she was about to follow through the doorway into the smaller quarters next door, she bumped into a great furry pile.

"Wo-o-of." The sound vibrated as if it came from deep in a cave.

Mary knew she'd disturbed one of John Goodman's dogs. As cramped as the Pilgrims were, John brought this immense mastiff and his friendly spaniel along on the trip to

America. 'Twas a good thing the dogs behaved so well. That mastiff weighed as much as Mary, if not more.

Early on, when some of the men argued that there would be no room for the dogs or that John should lodge them with the livestock, he simply looked at the men for a long time and silently gestured with his open hand toward their wives and children.

"As if he equates our families with his dogs," sputtered Master Martin, practically quivering with indignation.

But no one argued—and a good thing it was, for the children loved to play with the dogs. Ofttimes Mary looked over to see one of the little boys curled up, sleeping against the mastiff. *Everyone needs to find a comforting place, even if 'tis cuddled into a mountain of a dog.*

But for now, the dogs foiled Mary's plan. *Why am I so determined to find Elder Brewster?* True, she always admired him. Quiet, confident, and strong—that is how Mary would describe him. Thinking of Elder Brewster made Mary realize how she missed Fear. Mary knew 'twas why she longed to see Elder Brewster. The message from Fear needed to be given to her father.

As Mary sat stroking the soft fur of the mastiff, she saw Mistress Brewster come back to her bunk. Mary looked down and noticed a dusting of flour on the deck leading toward the door down into the hold. Mistress Brewster had been kneading dough before she went down.

Mary stood up and followed the almost invisible flour trail. It brushed down the ladder and through one storeroom and into another. It stopped right at the edge of a stack of ale barrels.

Mary wedged herself in the crevice and began humming a psalm. When no one seemed to be around, she whispered, "Elder?"

No answer.

"Elder, 'tis me, Mary Chilton." She whispered, hardly making a sound. "I promised Fear I would deliver a message for her."

Still no answer. Mary heard a scratching sound. Could it be scurrying rats? No. Mary caught a rhythmic pattern to the scratches. Aye, the elder hid here.

Mary hummed another snippet of song. In the middle, she whispered Fear's message. "As we left Holland, Fear asked that I tell you she loves you." It sounded like the psalm-singing the Pilgrims did, with the words being spoken and then sung. Mary hummed another line of the song before she delivered the next part. "She reassures you that she shall care for things in Holland."

Mary stood up and walked around the cramped store-room just in case someone watched. She set about humming and said, "Fear commits to walk with our Lord. She longs to follow to America as soon as you send word."

Mary turned to go toward the ladder.

"Thank you. God grant thee well, Mary."

The words were so faint she could barely hear them, but, having delivered the message, Mary felt a new lightness. *There, Fear. We've mended the weaving of the Brewster family just a little. May God comfort you as He comforted your father.*

5
A Vast and Furious Ocean

*A*ngry words swirled around the ship.

Captain Jones stomped up to the wheel, still yelling. "I shall lose my ship. And for what, I ask you? For a pious bunch of psalm-singers and their stowaway leader!"

The *bosun* warned the sailors. "Leave Master Jones be, lads. Ye don't want to cross paths with the captain in this kind of mood."

One sailor—the one who had first yelled at Mary and her friends—could not bear to leave it alone. "Throw 'em overboard, Cap'n!" he yelled up to the quarterdeck. "Throw the whole lot o' them puke-stockings overboard."

From below, he could not see the angry cloud building on the face of the ship's master.

"We got their money." The sailor spat in the wind. "They just be cargo, and when cargo gets troublesome a body needs to toss it overboard. Let 'em be food for the fishes."

"Bosun,"—the captain clipped his words, as he looked

hard at the sailor—"take Mr. Stubbs to the poop deck and explain the care we take with our cargo, no matter how troublesome."

Despite the captain's reassurance, the sailor's words frightened Mary.

That morning had started out so fair. She and her friends had walked on deck early. As they rounded the galley, they caught sight of Deacon Carver, Master Martin, and Elder Brewster walking into the captain's quarters.

"Was that Elder Brewster?" Elizabeth shook her head as if she were dreaming. "How did he board the ship in the middle of the ocean?"

"Shhh, Elizabeth," Mary said absently. She heard the captain bellow. *What will he think of this stowaway?*

"What is happening?" Constance looked confused.

The yelling had continued behind the closed door while Mary told Constance about Elder Brewster. The door slammed open, and the captain stomped out of the cabin.

Not long after the sailor's outburst, Elder Brewster and the other men made their way onto the deck, greeting everyone warmly. Mary and the girls followed as he climbed down into the main cabin and grabbed both Love and Wrestling in a huge bear hug. Mistress Brewster's smile wiped all the worry off her face.

"I see they did not manage to throw you overboard, William," his wife said, laughing like a girl.

"'Twas not for want of the idea," the elder said with a laugh. "But we are well on our way, and Captain Jones does not have a choice if he hopes to make landfall before winter. The English will be well pleased that I vanished. As long as I stay out of Merrie Old England, they will do nothing to bring me back."

Mary's father put an arm around Elder Brewster's shoulder and said, "By God's grace, William Brewster, you are safe. 'Twas a worry how much longer your secret could have been kept from the crew, much less curious passengers."

Mary blushed, but Elder Brewster smiled directly at her and winked.

"Aye, but some of those curious passengers brought God's own comfort to a lonely stowaway," he said.

Elder Brewster bent his knee, and all the Pilgrims did the same. Right there in the close quarters of the tiny ship, they prayed and sang psalms of praise.

As they gathered topside for their Sabbath service, Mary flinched to see the profane sailor by the name of Stubbs, hanging back, grinning and making slashing gestures across his throat toward the children. Because of his own strength and brawn, he enjoyed taunting the weak and the sick and frightening the children.

When Elder Brewster spoke with him about it, he cursed and swore even more bitterly. Mary remembered his earlier suggestion that all the passengers be thrown overboard. He told the elder that when they were tossed to the fishes, he would "make merry with what they had."

Strangely enough, there was only one crew member to die at sea—and it was that grinning sailor. He was perfectly fine in the morning, going about his work with a whistle and a swagger, and by afternoon he stumbled onto the deck, clutching his stomach. He died right there on the ship. The captain held a burial at sea.

The prosperous winds and fair weather continued a few days longer. It was not long after the captain noticed a wall of black on the horizon that the pitching and rolling of the ship intensified. Many of the passengers became violently seasick. Elizabeth, Mary, and Constance helped those who were sickest. Before long the air in the tight cabin soured from the sickness. Mary climbed down to the storeroom to get water. The *cooper,* John Alden, helped fill her bucket from one of the barrels.

"Be sparing of the water, Mary," he said. "We have precious little."

"I need to soak rags to wipe faces."

"Take the bucket for now, but we may have to use salt water if 'tis not for drinking. Because we lost the *Speedwell,* we have many more passengers than we planned."

As Mary climbed back up the ladder she had to loop her left arm around the ladder and hang on tight. The ship tossed and fell violently. Keeping the water from sloshing out of the bucket and keeping her own balance at the same time took concentration, and she could only do it one step at a time. As she moved into the main quarters, she could hear the *bosun* yelling orders into the howling wind up on deck.

"You there! Furl that canvas and wrap it tight. This storm builds, and there be nothing to do but ride it out."

Water poured into the cabin from the grating of the hatch.

"Quick!" The *bosun* yelled at the top of his voice and, even then, he could barely be heard. "Batten the hatches! Secure the longboat!"

One sailor yelled down into the main quarters, "Douse all your cooking fires and snuff out your candles. No fire until the sea calms."

Another torrent of icy water splashed in from the deck above them. The creaking timbers deafened those below.

"Tie down anything that will roll," the sailor finished.

Mary saw some of the men get up to secure the barrels and boxes, but by now few were feeling well enough to stand. Constance held a whimpering Damaris.

Elizabeth curled up in the corner of her mattress and moaned.

Mary struggled to keep her stomach from lurching. What was it about the violent pitching and rolling that made one so sick? Soon the entire cabin seemed to be writhing in the agony of seasickness. *One hundred and two passengers,* thought Mary, *and every one of them sick.* The rank air did not help.

If only I could go up on deck, Mary thought, but the roar of the wind and the violence of the storm made that impossible. She shivered from the intense cold. Not a sliver of light penetrated the cabin, since tarpaulins covered the grate they called the hatch. Mary wondered if this is what it felt like to be sealed into a coffin.

Time passed. The moans and retching increased with every hour. Mary felt queasy but nowhere near as bad as most of the passengers. An older girl named Priscilla and Mistress White helped Mary wipe faces with water-soaked rags dipped over and over in the bucket Mary had carried up to the cabin.

Vomit mixed with cold salt water ran across the deck, soaking the mattresses that lay on the floor. Those tending the sick slipped in the slime.

Dr. Fuller, the Pilgrims' doctor and surgeon, pulled himself up off his bunk. He made Mistress White go to her bunk because of her condition. "If she falls, she could injure her child and hasten its birth." He ended up yelling orders over the roar of the ocean.

He instructed John Alden to go below and bring hardtack back up. Mary helped pass the small pieces of crackerlike bread to everyone. It was so dark she had to locate people by feel. Priscilla and John gave tiny sips of water, wiping mouths as they went.

"Just eat tiny bites of hardtack and take only a sip of water at a time. Try to get your stomach used to taking food without weighing it down." The doctor paused, attempting to bring his own stomach under control.

Mary heard the creak of bunk ropes over near the Brewsters. She saw the flicker of a tiny candle flame.

"Dear friends, let me read to you," yelled Elder Brewster over the roar of the wind. He paused to gain strength. "I read from the One Hundred Seventh."

He cleared his throat. "Oh that men would praise the Lord for his goodness, and for his wonderful works to the children of men! And let them sacrifice the sacrifices of thanksgiving, and declare his works with rejoicing." He paused as the ship *heeled* dangerously far and a box went scudding across the deck.

He continued, "They that go down to the sea in ships, that do business in great waters; these see the works of the

Lord, and his wonders in the deep. For he commandeth, and raiseth the stormy wind, which lifteth up the waves thereof. They mount up to the heaven, they go down again to the depths: their soul is melted because of trouble." He stopped reading when a drenching torrent of water doused his flickering candle.

He lighted it and began again. "They reel to and fro, and stagger like a drunken man, and are at their wits' end. Then they cry unto the Lord in their trouble, and he bringeth them out of their distresses. He maketh the storm a calm, so that the waves thereof are still. Then are they glad because they be quiet; so he bringeth them unto their desired haven. Oh that men would praise the Lord for his goodness, and for his wonderful works to the children of men! Let them exalt him also in the congregation of the people, and praise him in the assembly of the elders."

He closed his Bible and doused the flame.

"Lord, we are at our wits' end," he prayed. "Calm the storm. Calm our fears. Amen."

Someone from the far end of the room—maybe it was William Bradford—raised a weak voice and began a psalm of thanksgiving. Others joined in. The ship still tossed, the fierce winds howled, and the fearful dark closed in around them, but once again the Pilgrims' hearts remembered their eternal security.

❧ ❧ ❧ ❧

Aside from fear, perhaps the smells and the closeness of the main cabin affected the passengers most. Normally people bathed at least once a season and washed their linens weekly, but since setting out in July, there had been little opportunity to bathe or wash linens. Cramped as they were, the natural odors that were barely noticed out of doors intensified below deck.

Mary tucked the handkerchief carrying her handful of Delft dirt into her pouch. When the smells became overpowering, she held the hankie to her nose and inhaled the earthy smell of Dutch soil.

The storm continued lashing the ship. After days of being confined to quarters with no chance to even empty buckets or *chamber pots,* some of the passengers were half frantic for a breath of fresh air.

Mary noticed John Howland. He began pacing the deck in the dark. At first he bumped from crate to chest to bunk, but eventually he learned his path in the dark. As the days dragged on, he took to sitting on the ladder near the hatch, despite the water that seeped in.

One day, they heard a rush of wind and water and momentary light, and then it darkened down again. John Alden said he thought the tarp covering the hatch must have blown loose. No one missed John Howland.

Many hours later, the same light and water rushed in, but this time the *bosun* entered with a bundle slung over his shoulder. As soon as the men below deck could make out that 'twas a body, they rushed to help.

"By all rights this man ought to be sleeping in the deep, but here he be." The *bosun* lowered the shivering, retching, body to the deck.

"'Tis John Howland. What happened?" Elder Brewster asked.

"I see the hatch cover flap back, and out comes this bloke." The *bosun* pointed to John. "I tell him to get back. 'Tis not safe. Even the helmsman must lash himself to the wheel—the seas are sweeping across the decks, and some of the swells cover the tops of the masts. When 'tis this bad, there's nothing to do but drift in the hands of God."

"But what about Howland?" Elder Brewster asked.

"He says, 'I must breathe air.' And before I can send him back, a wave comes crashing across the bow and sweeps the man into the churning sea."

"God have mercy." The elder was clearly shaken.

"Indeed He did. I have never seen such a thing in all my years at sea. When a man goes overboard in a storm, 'tis a natural burial at sea." The *bosun* shook his head. "But your man here . . . we look back and there he is hanging on to the line from the *topsail*. The waves battered him something fierce, but he hung on tight to that *topsail halyard*, and we used the *boathook* and managed to haul him in."

Those gathered around John Howland were speechless. God had spared John's life. It reminded Mary that the Lord still watched over them all.

"The man's still half dead, but he may pull out of it—he has pluck." The *bosun* turned to the coughing, sputtering Howland, "Fare thee well, young man."

The *bosun* turned to go topside when a scream ripped through the cabin.

"Mother?" Mary heard the fear in Constance's voice.

"What now?" asked the *bosun*.

"It appears that our wee babe chooses to be born in the middle of the ocean during the fiercest of storms." Master

Hopkins moved over to his wife with a crease between his eyebrows that belied his easy words.

"Good Lord! I shall leave you to it. Carry on." The *bosun* nearly ran up the ladder and through the hatch. The tarp was battened down once more.

Mary's mother and Priscilla readied the bed for John Howland while some of the men helped remove his sopping clothes. The roar of the wind still deafened them; children still cried; those stricken with seasickness, including Mary's father, still moaned on their bunks, but somehow, everyone knew that they had witnessed a miracle.

Master Hopkins pulled the canvas around the Hopkins's bunk space, and Dr. Fuller asked Mary to bring a bucket of seawater and to clean the area. Damaris whimpered as Constance took her across the cabin, near Elizabeth and the Tilleys. Mary did the best she could and withdrew to wait with her friends.

Mistress Hopkins labored through the night. In the morning, Mary wakened to the sound of a lusty cry.

"'Tis a boy, Mary." Constance hugged her friend. She looked so relieved.

"A boy with excellent lungs." Mary saw this as another sign that God continued to care for them. "What did you name him?"

Constance laughed her deep, rich laugh. "You'll not believe it—they named him Oceanus."

Mary laughed as well. As the ocean came crashing over the deck again she said, "I wonder how they ever found that name?"

The winds and the waves continued to lash the ship. Many times she *heeled* so far over that Mary could sense the one breath that would send the ship toppling into the deep. So far, each time they touched that angle of no return, Mary felt a hesitation—a pause—followed by the backward slip as the ship righted herself.

The creaking and groaning of the ship became as familiar as breathing to the passengers, so one day when they heard an ominous splitting sound, every head turned toward the timber above them. Like the shot of a cannon the timber cracked and buckled. A wild torrent of salt water crashed in on the Pilgrims from the break. The hatch flew open immediately, battens flying and ropes swinging. Captain Jones and the ship's officers clambered below deck to survey the damage.

The noise of the massive timber snapping terrified the passengers, but 'twas not until they saw the face of the captain that they fully understood the dire outlook.

"Perchance the *Mayflower* has sailed her last voyage, men," Captain Jones said. "Get a strong timber to brace under this broken beam and another to wedge as a prop, though I cannot see how we can make this ship seaworthy. That timber is the one that supports the main mast."

The little band of Pilgrims knew well what that meant. So did Mary. Pushing aside some of the bundles of Chilton belongings, she cleared a place to sit among them. She reached into the chest and took out the tightly packed bundle containing the gift from Isabella. Her plan had been to open it when they reached their new home on America's shore. She turned the package over, fingering the stiff texture of the oilcloth covering. *Perchance the package will never be opened,* she realized.

6

Mutiny on the Mayflower

The men ran to get the timbers, but the weight of the mast above the timber was too great to allow them to push the timber back into place. Hopelessness filled the room.

"Wait! What about the great screw?" asked Deacon Carver with sudden excitement.

"Aye," Elder Brewster said, pointing out men. "John Alden, Myles Standish, Stephen Hopkins, Richard Warren—move the crates and bring the screw."

Captain Jones merely shook his head, but Mary had seen them use the massive jack that they called an iron screw in Holland to raise the timber on a barn. She put her package back in the chest and jumped up to watch. *Dear God, please let it work. We've come through so much already.*

The wooden case holding the huge screw was placed on the floor directly under the broken beam, and the men began turning the wheel that moved the screw upward. The screw was bigger around than a man's upper arm. With each twist of

the wheel, it extended higher above the platform. When it hit
the bracing beam, the men kept turning, and it kept pushing
tighter and tighter—far beyond what they had been able to
accomplish with the wedge. Mary could see the groaning ship
beam begin to knit back together. The torrent of water
slowed to a trickle and finally stopped altogether. No one ut-
tered a word until Elder Brewster raised his arms and voices
raised in a psalm of thanksgiving.

"Well, I shall be jiggered," Captain Jones said as he shook
his head in wonder and walked all around the repair. He waited
until the singing and prayers were offered, then he formally
offered his gratitude to each man who helped save his ship.

The storm finally blew itself out. The Pilgrims first noticed the quiet. 'Twas almost like the hush of a Sabbath service. The pitch and roll of the ship lessened until the motion
became little more than a gentle rocking. They knew the
worst was over when sailors removed the batten from the
hatch and light streamed in below.

Many passengers were too weak to leave their beds, including Mary's father, but those who could undertook the
task of cleaning the main quarters. The girls worked until
their arms ached, scrubbing, emptying, airing, and tidying.
As they made trip after trip above deck emptying buckets
over the side, their eyes ached from the light. Mary wondered
how long they had drifted during the storm. Because they had
lived in utter darkness, they lost track of time. It could have
been a week, or it could have been three weeks. They had
been at sea for sixty-six days, not accounting for all the false
starts, according to Captain Jones.

The startling thing to Mary was that she had learned a

lesson in what Mother called "casting all your cares on the Lord." At first she feared they should all die, but day after day, she learned to take those fears and cry out to God. Like her mother, she found comfort. She longed to tell her mother about it, but first the work must be done.

Mary's mother spent her time with Father. His weakness kept him in bed below deck.

Dr. Fuller's young helper, William Butten, remained the weakest. The doctor stayed with him much of the time, but one morning Dr. Fuller awakened to find William dead. All the passengers mourned the hopeful young man. As the Elder Brewster and the passengers committed his body to the ocean, they looked up to see gulls circling ahead. Could that mean the *Mayflower* neared land?

Four days later, the Pilgrims awoke to a cry from the lookout, "Land ahoy!"

Pulling *breeches* over nightshirts and slipping into waist-coats as fast as they could fasten, button, and tie, the rumpled band of travelers scrambled up the ladder onto the deck. The women and girls tucked their cotton shifts into petticoats and waistcoats and were not far behind. Far in the distance, off the starboard bow, they spied a ribbon of land bathed in the early glow of sunrise. Mary, Constance, and Elizabeth huddled close together—feeling all shivery.

It took a long time for the passengers to believe it was land they saw, but when the dark strip came into focus many of them fell to their knees to give thanks. Some of Mary's fellow shipmates wept openly. The hardship of the voyage was etched on their gaunt faces.

"It does not seem real somehow," said Mary. "So difficult has been the task of getting here, it hardly seems possible that we draw close to the New World."

"Aye," Elizabeth said. "I expected to perish in the storm."

"And I," Constance agreed. "Now that landfall draws near—after all we've lived through, 'twould seem as if there would be more fanfare, more excitement!"

"Truth be told, I can do without any more excitement for a while." Elizabeth laughed.

"Do you know what I want?" Constance asked, without waiting for an answer. "I want a deep, long drink of fresh, cold water." What little water left had been stale and *brackish* for weeks now. Lately, they drank only ale. "So much water that it will run down my chin."

"Oh, aye! And fresh water to wash clothes and bathe and wash hair and . . . "

Elizabeth interrupted Mary. "Surely you don't plan to bathe. 'Tis almost winter!"

"I do indeed plan to bathe," Mary said. "I long to wash away all the ship smell. I want to scrub my linens and let them dry in the sunshine." Even though it was a cold November day, the early morning sun still shone on the water, and she could dream of warm sunshine.

Mary stayed at the rail for the longest time. She viewed the sliver of America with a hushed feeling of awe—almost as if she should not speak for a time. She remembered back to the service of Solemn Humiliation Pastor Robinson had held in Holland all those months ago. That day connected to this day.

"I shall leave you two on deck to watch the land grow ever closer," Mary teased. "I need to go tell my mother and father."

Mary climbed below deck. She found her mother sitting on a crate beside Father. Since his weakness increased, Mother spent more and more time by his side. As the days passed, his gums became red and blistered, and his teeth loosened. Mary overheard one sailor whisper something like *"scurvy"* to another.

"Mother, why don't you go on deck for a while. The shore grows ever closer. You look fair pale. I shall sit with Father for a time."

"Thank you, Mary. I shall do that. I long to walk and breathe some fresh air." Her mother kissed her and teasingly touched a new freckle on Mary's nose. It was an old game they had played since England days.

When Mary's mother left, Mary sat on the crate beside her father. She pushed aside her apron and dug in her pouch to remove the hankie with the Dutch soil. So much had happened in the four months since she said good-bye to her sisters and to Fear. England and Holland lay so far behind.

She remembered back to the time the Leyden boys split Father's head open with a rock. That day she found out they planned to travel to the New World. Mary closed her eyes. *God of heaven, we draw so near to America—the New World that called my father away from home and family. Now look at him. He can barely raise his head. Lord, can this be?*

Mary opened her eyes to see her father looking at her. "Father, do you need something to drink?"

"No, Mary." He lifted a hand to her face and put it against

her cheek, but he was so weak, she had to put her hand over his to keep it there.

"You wonder whether we should have ever started out, don't you?" He coughed and winced with the pain it caused.

"With you so sick, Father, and my sisters left behind, doubt creeps in sometimes," she said truthfully. "Leyden seems so far away." She wondered how Father always seemed to know what she was thinking.

He dropped his hand back onto the bed, but Mary still covered it with her own. Each day the weakness increased.

"God called us to make this journey, Mary." A momentary flash in his eyes lit up his face. "Of that I am certain. I would *lief* die in this wild land of freedom than live in a land where worshiping God be a crime. And Holland . . ." He started coughing.

"Father, don't talk if it makes you cough."

He finished coughing and started back where he left off. "In Holland, 'twas not just the lack of financial promise that convinced me. 'Twas that the people seemed so content with a half-hearted commitment."

Mary took the cloth and wiped the fever off his face.

"Our people hungered to know God. We longed to dig deeply into the Scriptures and let them change us." He sighed and paused.

At first Mary thought he dozed, but she could feel a tension in his hand.

"Daughter, I understood how you always longed to belong. I recognized it because I also felt that deep longing, but . . . 'tis not a longing for place or even for family."

"But, Father—"

"Let me finish while I have breath, little one."

"Aye."

"Some call that feeling the inconsolable longing, but no matter what you call it, someday you will find your true home. The wonder will be that it has nothing to do with England or Holland or America or even with our family." He paused to slow his labored breathing.

"But I don't understand." She didn't like this conversation.

"I know, Mary, but you will." He touched her cheek lightly with the curve of his knuckles. "I pray you will."

Mary sat on the crate, waiting for her mother to return—feeling even more confused and frightened. Her throat felt as if someone's hands tightened around it. *I want to go home. I want things to be like they were before with Mother, Father, Isabella, Ingle, and Christian.* Homesickness swept over her. *If we were still in Holland we'd be strapping on our skates and gliding down the canals. The storks would be gone until the thaw, the bulbs would be tucked under the frozen soil, and the hodgepodge would be simmering on the fire, and—*

"Mary, did your father wake at all?" Her mother's question brought her back to the *Mayflower.*

"Aye. He talked to me for a time." Mary stood up to let her mother sit down.

"'Tis good," her mother said. "He wanted to talk with you."

Mary climbed up the ladder, but before she even got on deck she heard loud voices raised in argument.

"Mary, come." Constance motioned her over. She and Elizabeth sat on crates pushed up against the rail.

"Why the angry voices?" Mary asked.

"It started earlier when Captain Jones told the men that the storm blew us off course. We are nowhere near Virginia or the Hudson River. We are far north of that in the area they call New England," Elizabeth explained. "I think he said they called that piece of land Cape Cod. Is that right, Constance?"

"Aye. The elder and the others want us to stay aboard the *Mayflower* while Captain Jones runs along the coast to the south toward the Virginia lands," Constance said.

"Stay aboard?" Mary longed to get off the ship, and she couldn't hide the disappointment in her voice.

"Some of the young Strangers and the servants feel the same way," said Constance.

"They began to complain, and one declared that because they were not in Virginia, they were in free territory. He tries to convince the others that the rules no longer apply to them," Elizabeth said, her voice filled with dismay.

One young Stranger raised his voice so all could hear. "The *patents* we carry are for Virginia. The king has no *jurisdiction* over us here." He punctuated his words with a fist raised in the air. "I say we go ashore and we take our liberty and that we be servants no longer. Neither shall we be bound like the others to work for the company what sent us."

In the middle of the shouting, one of the sailors yelled up to Captain Jones, "Master, we be finished with this *mewling* bunch of whiners!"

Another chimed in. "Aye. Set the whole lot of them ashore and let us return to England while we still have sufficient food supplies."

Mary knew that she and her friends ought to go below deck, but it seemed better to stay put than to get into the middle of the trouble. Discontent and anger simmered. Mary did not relish seeing it reach the boiling stage.

Master Jones stood on the quarterdeck and called down with a commanding tone, "Elder Brewster, Deacon Carver, Master Bradford, Captain Standish. Please join me in my cabin." He turned around to face the angry young travelers and his own seaman. "If any man of you so much as says another word before I give you leave, you shall return to England in chains. That is—if I don't decide to feed your carcass to the fish in the meantime."

A temporary silence descended on the ship, and Constance poked the girls with a signal that they should go below deck.

All the women below seemed worried as they went about their chores. But no matter how tense things might become, babies still cried; people got hungry; and the sick needed tending.

Constance took Damaris, and the girls rounded up the other little ones and led them into a corner to play while trouble brewed all around them. Mary gathered buckets and scraps of linen so the little ones could pretend to put their *poppets* to bed. They had great fun putting a *poppet* in the bucket and covering it with a blanket and pulling it out again. Then two *poppets* might go into the same bucket. Sometimes the bucket was turned over to make a house. The children played at this game until the noon hour and time for dinner.

Though the families cooked and ate separately, the chatter of mealtimes could normally be heard throughout the cabin. Not this time. Everyone ate in silence. The men closeted with Captain Jones did not return for dinner.

"Do you think the men will mutiny against the leaders?" Elizabeth asked after the little ones finally napped on a mattress.

"I don't know," Constance said. "But those men spent many hours speaking with my father about the mutiny aboard the *Sea Venture*."

"'Tis serious enough by the looks on the faces of those who went into the Captain's quarters." Mary wished she were back in Holland basting *interfacing* to bodices and—

She stopped herself mid-thought. *Shame on you! Think of Fear, all alone in Leyden. At least you have your mother and father with you. Didn't you decide that home is where your parents are? So, Mary Chilton, your home is right here on the Mayflower.* Though she talked sternly to herself, her stomach still churned like the treacherous sea they had just crossed.

7
The Bleak
Sandy Shore

John Alden, summon all the men to assemble in the Great Cabin," Elder Brewster said. "Include everyone from Master Martin to the servants, Saints to Strangers."

Mary and her mother watched as the men who had been below deck solemnly lined up to climb to the upper deck and make their way to the quarterdeck. Father's weakness kept him from joining the men.

"Mother, what do you suppose will happen?"

"I do not know, Mary. What I do know is that we can trust William Brewster. He seeks God in everything." Her mother leaned against the bunk.

"You look tired."

"Aye. The voyage takes its toll on us all." Mother seemed beyond weary.

"But land is nearly within reach; we are almost home." Mary very nearly repeated those last two words. *Almost home.* Had she ever thought of America as home before? Could it be that the thin strip of land off the starboard bow was to be her forever home—a place where they could worship as they pleased and till the soil and—

"Mary, you do know that the storm blew us far north, do you not? And that Captain Jones sails south even now to try to reach Virginia?" Mother took a cloth and dipped it in the bucket of *brackish* water to wipe Father's face.

Aye, Mary did know.

"Indeed, even when we anchor, Captain Jones offered to allow us to live aboard the *Mayflower* till we build shelter. He decided not to attempt the ocean crossing back to England until spring."

"Stay on the *Mayflower?* Oh, Mother, no!" Mary could not bear to think of staying on the *Mayflower* for months more. "'Tis cruel to be so close to the end of our journey and yet have to stay aboard."

"Nothing changes." Her mother laughed. "From the time you were a babe, we no sooner set out on a journey but you would be asking, 'Are we there yet?' Nay, Mary, nothing changes."

Mary felt impatient from the top of her head to the tips of her toes. How she longed to dig her toes in dirt again, to feel tree branches scrape against her arms, to smell the scent of lilies, to hear the buzz of insects, to taste wild berries . . .

"Mary?"

"Sorry, Mother. You are right. I *am* impatient."

Father turned and moaned, and mother tried to wipe some of the heat off his face. His thrashing uncovered his leg and Mary gasped to see the swelling of his joints and the sores opening on his flesh.

She longed to run away, but instead she took the bucket to dump the lukewarm water and get fresh. On her way downstairs, she saw Constance with wee Oceanus. *How can one vessel hold birth and death all at the same time? Death? . . . Why did I say death?*

"How goes it, Mary?" Constance sounded happy as always.

"Truth be told, Constance, I am fair sick of this tiresome ship."

"Oh, fiddle! This shall be the adventure of our lives. When we have nothing but grizzled gray hair, we shall still be talking about the *Mayflower*. Do you not remember how excited we were to finally set sail from England?"

"Aye." Mary paused, hating to deflate her friend's joy. "Father does not improve, and I fear for his life. Perchance he was too old for this journey."

"I am sorry, Mary." Constance shifted the baby to one arm so she could put her other arm around her friend. "What manner of friend am I that I did not see that?"

"A good friend—that's what manner of friend. Everyone on the ship has felt poorly, 'tis just that now they've all recovered, and Father has not." Mary shook off her worry. "I need to think of something else."

"Would you care to hold the ocean in your hands?"

"The ocean?"

"Well, not exactly the whole ocean—" Constance laughed again "—but a wee bundle called Oceanus."

Mary giggled and took Constance's little brother. As the baby nuzzled into Mary's neck, she felt comforted.

"So what can the men do all this time in the Great Cabin?" Mary asked.

"Father said they were crafting a document. Elder Brewster wanted to bind all together for the common good before they ever set foot on land."

Constance was right. Several hours later the men filed out of the captain's quarters, and Elder Brewster assembled all who were well enough and read the document that they prepared. Mary was glad that her father had been able to sign the document as well.

"In the name of God, amen." The elder paused and looked around at all those gathered in the twilight. "We, whose names are underwritten, the loyal subjects of our dread sovereign Lord, King James, by the grace of God, of Great Britain, France, and Ireland, king, defender of the faith, et cetera."

Mary looked over at Constance and caught her eye. Never would they forget this solemn gathering—surely Constance would gather this moment into her collection of gray-haired memories.

Elder Brewster continued to read in his deep resonant voice. "Having undertaken for the glory of God, and advancement of the Christian faith and honor of our king and country, a voyage to plant the first colony in the Northern parts of Virginia, do by these presents, solemnly and mutually in the presence of God and one of another, covenant and combine ourselves together into a civil body politick . . ." He took a breath and continued. ". . . for our better ordering and preservation, and furtherance of the ends aforesaid: and by virtue hereof, to enact, constitute, and frame such just and equal laws, ordinances, acts, constitutions, and offices, from time to time, as shall be thought most meet and convenient for the general good of the colony unto which we promise all due submission and obedience. In witness whereof we have hereunder subscribed our names at Cape Cod the eleventh of November, in the reign of our sovereign Lord, King James of England, France, and Ireland, the eighteenth, and of Scotland the fifty-fourth. Anno Domini 1620."

The elder finished reading the document he called the Mayflower Compact just as Captain Jones came up to speak with him. Some of the Pilgrims went below deck, but Mary stayed.

"There be no way to navigate Tucker's Terror." The captain spoke to Elder Brewster and the Pilgrims' newly elected governor, Deacon Carver.

"Tucker's Terror?"

"Aye, a treacherous riptide that will likely cast us up against the shoals. Champlain mapped it in 1605 and pronounced it impassable. Until now I questioned his statement, but look over the starboard bow." He pointed to a rocky stretch of water. "'Twould be folly to attempt the passage to Hudson and Virginia as you directed. I shall head back to Cape Cod tonight and anchor there."

Governor Carver nodded his head. "We need to take on fresh water and repair the shallop." The shallop was a small sailing boat that could be either sailed or rowed. It was perfect for coastal exploration. The Pilgrims brought it along, dismantled and stored between the decks. They needed to haul it out, reassemble it, and repair the damage done by the storm and by weary travelers sleeping in the hull.

Mary watched the swirling water as the ship turned to head back to that bleak sandy shore on the very finger of Cape Cod.

Mary lifted Remember Allerton up to the rail to wave farewell to her father in the longboat as it pushed toward the tip of Cape Cod. This Saturday morning had dawned clear and cold—too cold to be on deck without being wrapped in woolen blankets. The chill in the air was the reason sixteen armed men now sailed toward shore. They needed firewood. Not a single stick remained on the ship, and the main cabin remained damp and icy cold. The cries of babies, the creak of the ship's timber, and the staccato sound of coughing filled the air.

Remember's little sister played alongside. To be safe, Mary tied her *leading strings* onto a *belaying pin* so she could enjoy the fresh air, yet stay safe from climbing.

"How does Mistress Allerton fare?" asked Elizabeth.

"She feels poorly much of the time. Mother thinks her time draws near," Mary said.

The longboat made a quick trip of it. Mary and her friends left the little ones with their mothers after dinner. Elizabeth stood at the rail with Mary as the boat approached the ship. Some of the men rowed, while the rest sat silent and watchful, holding their matchlock muskets upright beside them. The longboat held plenty of firewood, and Mary could see that while some gathered firewood, others must have been hunting. They unloaded a brace of wild duck and a bucket of clams. Coming aboard, Captain Standish reported to Captain Jones that they had not yet found fresh water.

Mary thought that, compared to what they did bring, the fresh water could wait.

Elizabeth twirled around. "Tonight we shall be warm and fall asleep with full bellies for once."

"Aye. I shall go below and fire up the *brazier*. I, for one, shall be happy to help with the cooking."

That night the smell of the juniper wood fires wafted though the cabin, sweetening and warming the air.

The following day was the Sabbath and, though many of the Strangers were anxious to set about exploring, the Saints insisted that day be spent in worship, meditation, and thanksgiving. The first thing Monday morning, however, Mary heard the shallop being unloaded. Excitement seemed to vibrate throughout the ship.

"Mary! We get to go. Get up and ready yourself."

"Elizabeth, what are you talking about?" Mary could tell from her friend's face an adventure loomed on the horizon. "Prepare for what?"

"Young Mistress Tilley is beside herself—you shall have to excuse her lack of particulars." Constance laughed her brightest laugh. "We three are among the very first chosen to set foot on American soil."

"All three of us?" Mary could hardly believe it.

"Aye. And what think you the goal of our merry party?" Constance enjoyed teasing above all else.

"Are we to help with the exploring?" Mary knew that could not be as soon as the words came out of her mouth.

"Nay."

"Will we be cooking for the explorers?"

"Nay!" This time Elizabeth and Constance said it together, both laughing and poking each other.

"Enough! Tell me. I need to make ready."

"One of us sounds a wee bit impatient," Constance teased. "The men are taking the shallop ashore to mend all the gaps that opened up during the storm. They agreed to take some of the women to do the wash."

"The wash? Our first day in America and we will do the wash?" Mary said. It figured. She laughed. Now this would be something to tell those someday grandchildren—the very first thing they did in the New World was scrub grubby shifts and drawers. Indeed, the washing had not been done since leaving England. This was no small job.

It took several trips of the longboat to ferry the laundry crew ashore along with the huge iron kettles and bundles of soiled linens. The last trip brought a boatload of children who had begged to be allowed to run and play.

Some of the men stood watch with their matchlock muskets loaded and ready. The big boys gathered firewood and built fires to heat the water in the kettles, while the women shaved lye soap into the water. When the water was hot enough, the actual washing, scrubbing, rinsing, and wringing began. 'Twas hard work, but Mary could see that the familiarity of doing wash pleased the women.

Mary, Elizabeth, and Constance played with the children, watching them run along the sand and roll down the sand dunes. Because John Goodman helped the men repair the shallop, his two dogs came along as well. The dogs ran along the shore, barking at crabs and birds and children. The children, in turn, threw sticks for the dogs to retrieve.

In between their play, the children all helped to wring out the wash and lay the pieces across bushes to dry.

When time came for dinner, the longboat rowed over to the *Mayflower* and picked up Desire Minter and Priscilla Mullins, who brought the noon meal—a delicious clam stew. *Trenchers* had to be shared, and the clean clamshells worked as scoops, but it all added to the festive feel of the day.

After lunch some of the wee children crawled up next to John Goodman's mastiff and fell asleep.

Mary looked over the assembled Pilgrims—many of whom she had known for her whole life. *Perhaps doing everyday chores is the true sign that we are home.*

She looked around this land. The men had climbed a hill and could see water on the other side of the land. They reported that this Cape Cod was a thin arm jutting out to sea. It did not matter to Mary. She knew that as it curled around, it was attached to America.

Yes, she could picture Mother, Father, and herself living in a cozy house here in this New World. Father had been right all along. Perhaps they needed to cross the vast Atlantic Ocean to find a land big enough to allow them to build a life and a church in which they could worship the Lord without fear of punishment.

All my life I yearned to belong. Heavenly Father, is this the place I hungered for? Did You plant a longing for this America in my heart? Mary turned to go help her friends, but she wished she had remembered to bring her oilcloth-wrapped bundle to open here in America.

8

Gunpowder and Buried Treasure

Someday, as we Pilgrims tell the story of our adventures to our children and grandchildren, the men will tell their tales of expeditions and explorations—of Indians and wolves—of near shipwrecks and finding buried treasure." Constance took the *trencher* out of the basin of water. "And what shall we tell?"

Elizabeth laughed. She loved seeing Constance in a temper.

"Indeed! We shall tell of washing *nappies*, of cooking meals on a tiny tin box, of *minding* babies and scrubbing stubborn puke stains off the deck."

Even Mary laughed. "I know why they named you Constance."

"Do tell, Mary," Elizabeth said, grinning at Constance.

"Because you constantly complain about your lot as a girl."

The three friends enjoyed their time together but, truth be told, they grew ever more restless to be out doing anything except tending and caring and cleaning.

Not that everything exciting happened off ship. The day Mary and her friends went ashore to do the wash, Francis Billington nearly blew the ship up. It didn't surprise Mary. Francis was a little older than she was, but trouble followed that boy everywhere. The Billington family hailed from London and joined the Pilgrims at the dock in Southampton. The *Mayflower* passengers had never seen such a fussing and fighting family. But it was the boy's fascination with guns and fire that caused the true uproar.

Francis had not been in the group that went ashore to do the wash. He stayed behind. As Mary and the girls returned to the ship—tired and satisfied after a long day of work mixed with play—they heard an enormous explosion followed by many smaller explosions. Water sloshed against the ship as the concussion rocked it violently. Smoke billowed out of the room where they stored the muskets and gunpowder, and a soot-streaked, burned Francis came screaming out the door, almost knocking Mary down.

Sailors and Pilgrims alike grabbed buckets of water to douse the flames, and an angry Governor Carver sat Francis down on a crate.

"Whatever did you do, Francis Billington?" the governor asked.

"Nothing," Francis lied as he blew on his hands to keep the burns from hurting as much.

"Ask Goodman Billington to come topside," Governor Carver said to John Alden. When the boy's father joined them the question was repeated.

"I only tried to make some squibs—them firecrackers you make out of feathers." Looking at the puzzled faces,

Francis explained. "I gathered the quills from them wild ducks we ate last night and filled 'em with gunpowder." He didn't seem to notice the gasps of the men listening. "I got the flints and lit the first one, but it only popped a little."

"You lit the gunpowder on my ship?" Captain Jones clipped the last consonant on every word.

"Aye. But when it fizzled, I tried to stuff more gunpowder into each squib. I got a bunch on the floor, but I figured I would sweep it up later."

No one said a word.

Francis continued, "No matter how much gunpowder I managed to press into the shaft, the explosions were no more than a pop, so I decided to shoot off one of them muskets as a joke—the ones up there were loaded with powder already. I figured inside this room it would make a loud noise and scare all the girls."

"You shot a musket in my powder room?" Captain Jones shook his head as if he could not believe what he heard. "With an open barrel of gunpowder?"

"Aye. But first I had to find some fuse, so I got a piece of candlewick from down below and lit it with the flint. I lit the gun, and it went off, but the gun jerked so hard, I dropped the wick, and it caught the spilled powder on fire and . . ."

"I cannot bear to hear any more." Captain Jones told Francis's father to take him below while they decided what to do.

Before the men left to decide how to deal with Francis, Elder Brewster bent his knee and thanked God for keeping them safe once again. Captain Jones seemed to agree that 'twas nothing short of a miracle that the keg of gunpowder did not ignite.

The next day Captain Standish mounted the first exploration. The shallop was far from finished, so they decided to undertake an overland expedition to the place that had what appeared to be a wide river running into the bay. Many expressions of concern followed the announcement, but the days grew colder and shorter. Every person aboard knew the disaster that lay ahead if they did not settle and build shelter before winter settled hard on the land. Governor Carver finally decided that because of the obvious dangers, the expedition would be "permitted rather than approved."

Mary joined Elizabeth and Constance at the rail as the two girls waved to their fathers in the longboat. They stood watching until the boat landed on the white sandy beach, and the sixteen men were put ashore. Wearing the shiny piece of body armor they called a *corselet*, the expedition set off, each man carrying his musket and sword. The girls watched until they could no longer even see the glint of sunlight off the metal armor.

"How I wish I could go with them," Constance said.

"What about the savages?" Elizabeth had heard her share of hair-raising tales about the Indians. When Captain John Smith of the Jamestown settlement returned to England, people could not get their fill of stories.

"I look forward to knowing more about the Indians," Mary said. "True, the stories make them sound *barbaric*, but I cannot help wondering how much is fact and how much is the stuff of storytellers and *bards*."

"'Tis true." Constance turned around and plopped on a crate. "After all, this is their land."

"Their land, aye . . . but our congregation also believes

God led us to occupy this same land," said Elizabeth. "If there are savages as some say . . ."

"Elizabeth speaks true. Years of praying came before we ever set foot on the *Mayflower*." Mary moved over to another crate and pulled her winter wrap closer. The weather seemed to get more chill with each day. If they were back in Holland, *Mevrow* van Altvorst would be lifting some of her more tender plants and muttering about a killing frost.

That reminded Mary of Holland. "Remember when we first came to Holland? The Dutch folk seemed so scary to me. They talked funny, and they were always bustling around in those wooden shoes. Clomp, clomp, clomp. I shall never forget the sound of their *klompen* on the tile floors and cobbled streets. And in the winter, when they strapped their skates to their shoes and took off . . . I became terrified. As a three-year-old, I could make no sense of them, and they frightened me. I spent my first year in Leyden plastered to my mother's leg." Mary laughed at the memory. "Poor Mother. She spent her days hobbled at the knee by my fear."

Elizabeth laughed at the picture that made. She pushed Constance over to make room to sit on her crate.

"Mary, I had not thought about the strangeness being part of the fear. When I lived in England, everyone feared the gypsies. They said gypsies stole children right out of their yards—especially children with light hair like mine." Constance tucked a few of the windblown strands of blonde hair back under her *coif*, almost as if to hide the yellow color. "Now that I have grown, I see the folly of that threat. Why would the gypsies want more children? They could barely feed their own."

"So you think the Indians may be simple and good?" Elizabeth asked.

"I doubt that be true, since there must be something to the stories," Constance said thoughtfully. "Perchance it be somewhere in the middle. Some of the stories of savagery may be true, just as they are for our people. Other parts of the stories may just arise from lack of understanding."

"I do not think it wise to let our guard down," Elizabeth said. "When Father's cousin came to America, he came up against some Indians a time or two."

"Nor do I," Mary agreed. "But Elizabeth spoke true when she remembered all the prayers offered for this journey—in fact, our families and congregation across the ocean still pray for us."

"And?" Constance cocked her head in interest and raised that eyebrow of hers.

"And, who is to say that God, if we are indeed following His leading in coming here, is not, even now, working in the hearts of some of these who look like savages to us?"

"Now that is an interesting thought, Mary Chilton." Constance swung her legs around and stood up. "I need to help Mother with Damaris and the wee babe. Call out to me if anything exciting happens."

"What? Like Francis tries to blow us back to England?" Elizabeth also shook out her skirts.

"Please do not even make the suggestion," Mary said. "I shall go below deck and bide with Father awhile so Mother can breathe some fresh air."

After the party had been ashore for the best part of three days, the sailor manning the longboat caught the signal that the men had gathered on the beach. He rowed out to load the men and supplies and bring them back to the *Mayflower*. After supper that night, in the gently rocking main cabin of the *Mayflower* warmed with fragrant juniper wood fires, everyone gathered to hear the report of the exploration. Captain Jones joined them, as did several of the crew.

Captain Standish stood up in the center of the room, as if to give a starched report. He was a short man of ruddy complexion who held his body ramrod straight. His hair and beard were much the same color as Mary's coppery hair. "We had not been ashore more than an hour when we surprised six savages with a dog—"

"Nay, Captain Standish," Master Hopkins interrupted. "I saw only five."

Captain Standish bristled at the interruption but began again. "'Twas near a mile south, along the beach, that our party noticed five or six Indians and a dog." He paused to look at Master Hopkins, who nodded his head. "They spied us and disappeared into the woods, whistling their dog after them."

"We followed them, trying to catch their trail, but they seemed to disappear," William Bradford added with a quizzical shake of his head.

"You plunged into the forest after a pack of wild men?" Captain Jones spoke in that clipped way again. They recognized it as agitation. "How did ye not know 'twas a trap?"

Captain Standish sat down to answer slowly, "We had our weapons drawn, and our *corselets* protected our most vulnerable areas . . ." His discomfort was relieved when he was interrupted again.

"No matter," said Edward Tilley. "No one could say 'twas the wisest course of action, but the surprise of seeing them overrode our common sense."

The men took turns giving report. They never found the Indians. They did not even find tracks.

"We did find buried treasure," Master Hopkins said, looking at the children seated all around the deck.

"Buried treasure?" asked one of the boys, as he wiggled in anticipation of a story.

"Not Spanish doubloons from pirate ships but almost as good." Constance's father loved to tease as much as his daughter did.

"Tell!" rang out several voices almost at the same time.

"We came across a spring of fresh water . . ." He looked around at the children, hoping for some disappointment before going on. "But that was not the treasure."

No one interrupted.

"As we walked up a small hill, Captain Standish noticed some recently dug mounds. At first we thought they were fresh graves, but they appeared different. We dug down a ways and found a large basket . . ."

"What did you find inside?" Bartholomew Allerton knew never to interrupt his elders, but the thought of buried treasure overcame good manners to an eight-year-old boy.

"Look." Master Hopkins put Bartholomew's hands together, palm up, ready to hold treasure. The man reached into his pouch and spilled a handful of richly colored seeds into the boy's cupped hands.

"This is the treasure?"

"Aye. We found a whole basket of seeds for next year's crop of Indian corn. This treasure means we will have plenty to eat next harvest." Master Hopkins motioned to Bartholomew to pass some of the seeds around, so all the children could touch them.

One of the sailors hanging on the ladder turned to his friend and said in an overloud voice, "They *nicked* them seeds right out from under the savages' noses. There be grief to pay for that."

Elder Brewster furrowed his eyebrows. "Perchance the seed stash, laid right across our path, was God's provision for us. We brought seeds with us, but I fear that the climate and the soil may not agree with our English peas and our Dutch barley. The hours we spent in prayer may have been answered today."

"What about God's provision for them angry savages?" heckled the sailor.

"Lad," —it was the clipped voice of Captain Jones. "Perhaps you left some chores undone above deck." He did not have to repeat his suggestion. The two sailors scrambled up the ladder.

"The man raises a fair question. We made a covenant to come back next year and pay the Indians for their seed as well as replacing it." Elder Brewster paused. "'Tis to be hoped that the Indians bury their seed stores near several different fields, so that if animals raid one, they still have plenty."

The elder bent his knee, as did the rest of the company. He prayed, thanking God for His provision, for seeing them safely back to the ship, and asking for wisdom in their dealings with the Indians. Mary could tell that the elder struggled with the worry that what they saw as God's provision might belong to someone else. "Like Elijah's oil jar, Almighty God, and like the boy's lunch of loaves and fishes—multiply the seed. Make it sufficient for the Indians and make it sufficient for us as well. Amen."

The weather turned bitter, and ice formed on the top of buckets. With the shallop repairs complete about ten days later, a second expedition went out. The men decided to sail down to the mouth of the river they had found on the first expedition and replenish their water supply from the spring nearby.

Several of the passengers wanted to disembark and make their home right at the hill of Master Hopkins's "buried treasure," which they named Corn Hill. Mary often wondered if they had to spend so much time deciding where to set up their new home. It was taking so long. Couldn't they just pick a place and get started?

The leaders promised that when they came back from this expedition they would hold a meeting and decide whether to keep looking or whether to settle at Corn Hill.

After little more than a day, the shallop came sailing back with only a handful of the men who originally set out. Word spread all over the ship, and some thought the worst—that something had happened to their loved ones. Pilgrims gathered at the rail to see if their husband, father, or brother was on board.

As soon as the shallop came within earshot, the helmsman yelled out, "Ho, the ship! Bringing supplies."

Many a tear of gratitude fell to find out that the shallop was sent back to bring more seed stock and that the men were safely exploring. When they went back to Corn Hill they found even more seed. They brought back another ten bushels of Indian corn seed and some Indian wheat or maize seed, some dried beans, and even a bottle of oil—all had been *cached* on the hill. They wanted to get the seed to the ship before it froze so they sent it on ahead.

Another day passed, and those keeping watch on the *Mayflower* saw the signal fire on the beach—the sign to send the shallop for the return trip.

Before the men even returned, there was a flurry of excitement aboard the *Mayflower*. All the women hastened around the ship arranging for the return of the men, preparing for the meeting to decide where they would settle, and cooking a savory supper with some of the game that came back with the seed. All the women except for Mistress White, that is. Amid the bustle and twitter, the warm fires and the duck stew, Susannah White gave birth to a boy child. As those gathered heard him wail, someone remarked that he was the very first Pilgrim born after landfall in America. They named the baby boy Peregrine, which meant "one who has made the journey."

Mary's mother could not take part in the preparations—Father's illness kept her at his bedside. Only when Mary took a turn sitting with him did Mother have a chance to go above deck. Father stirred now and then, but a terrible weakness had overtaken him. Most of the others who suffered had since left their beds, and Mary continued to pray for her father's recovery.

That evening Mother came back and touched Mary on the shoulder. She had fallen asleep next to her father, and her head rested on the covers right next to him. As she carefully moved, trying not to wake him, she realized that at some time while she slept her father had moved his hand to stroke her hair. *Please, heavenly Father, most holy, heal my father.*

9

Almost There

As the Pilgrims gathered to discuss their settlement plans, it soon became clear that opinion was divided. The men told of finding an Indian dwelling and several Indian graves —one freshly dug. The river they had begun to call the Pamut River was not a river at all. It was a tidal estuary.

"This place be as good as any," one Pilgrim said. "'Tis but folly to go any later into the season without shelter."

"Aye. I shall grant you that." Governor Carver led the meeting. "Truth be told, however, the Pamut is too shallow for ships, as is the harbor. If we hope to have ships plying goods and passengers to and fro across the ocean, this cannot be our settlement."

"Corn Hill be a good defensible location," said another.

"True enough," William Bradford said. "But there is no water at Corn Hill. All our water would needs be hauled up from the springs. Can we defend a stronghold that stands to run out of water?"

"The fishing here in Cape Cod holds great promise. We should be able to salt down many barrels of cod to send back to England." This reasoning caused murmured agreement.

The debate went back and forth for a good long time with no accord.

From the back of the room, one of the ship's mates, Robert Coffin, spoke up. "Beggin' yer pardon, but, when I sailed here before, we anchored in at a good, deep harbor not far from here. We called it Thievish Harbor because one of the wild men what often hung around stole one of our harpoons." He paused. "I believe it be the harbor what John Smith calls Plymouth on the map."

Elder Brewster rolled out his copy of John Smith's 1614 map of the area and found the bay. The company of Pilgrims decided to make one more expedition to see Coffin's Thievish Harbor before coming to a decision.

Eighteen men set out the following Wednesday. This time Mary did not stand at the rail to see them off. 'Twas bitterly cold with a wind that cut right through clothing. The *Mayflower* pitched and rolled, and the spray froze on their hair and clothes.

Even below deck, the whistling wind through the cracks and the swirling draft blowing through the open grate made the main cabin blustery, chill, and damp. Coughing and sneezing kept time to cries of babies and whining pleas of toddlers. Teeth chattered and bellies rumbled from hunger.

Food had been scarce almost since they left England and, except for days when the men caught game, they went to bed hungry nearly every night. The last bit of meal grew so bug-infested that the young people took turns sifting out bugs so the grain could be used. The thought of it turned Mary's stomach. Now that winter descended on the land, hunting stopped. Wild game had either burrowed under or flown to warmer climes.

Sadness settled in with the onset of winter as well. Most of the women stayed busy with the work of caring for the sick ones along with their regular chores. Loneliness hit them all at one time or another, but some seemed to become lonelier and lonelier as time went on.

William Bradford and his wife, Dorothy, had made the decision to leave their small son with family in Leyden until they could settle and send for him. As Mistress Bradford helped with the little ones, Mary couldn't help seeing the loneliness in her.

Each time her husband left on an expedition, Mistress Bradford would walk the deck waiting to catch sight of the returning boat. While the weather was still fair, she often perched atop one of the crates and read a book—waiting. Now that the sea spray turned icy and the deck had become slick and slippery, she wrapped in blankets and tried to stay near the rail so she had a handhold.

The expedition had only been gone two days when Captain Jones came below deck. For the first time, he seemed shaken. "Where is Elder Brewster?"

"Here, Captain."

"I bring tragic news . . . William Bradford's wife slipped on deck and went over the port side into the icy water below." He shook his head from side to side as if he could not believe what he had seen.

"No!" the cries went up all over the cabin.

"So many blankets tangled around her . . . they soaked up water, becoming sodden and heavy. She slipped too fast beneath the water." He continued to shake his head. "Too fast."

Elder Brewster gathered the company of Pilgrims together, and they knelt to pray. How could they find words to tell William Bradford?

Mother still sat on the crate beside Father. Mary squeezed in to sit with her. *So much loss . . .*

"Mary, 'tis so difficult to say good-bye to friends." Mother held Mary's hand in both of hers.

Mary no longer knew what to say. Back in Holland, she yearned to find a place—somewhere to belong. Along the way, she realized that the place didn't matter as much as the people. She finally understood that as long as she had her family and friends, she had her home. Yet, one by one, she seemed to be losing family and friends. She longed for Isabella, Christian, Ingle, and Fear—all lost to her. And Mistress Bradford . . . slipping away . . . all alone.

Mary looked long at Father and accepted the truth she could not face till now. He lay closer to heaven than he did to earth. Did Mother know? Mary looked over to see tears spilling out of Mother's eyes onto the sleeve of Father's nightshirt. How would they let him go?

Mary remembered the words Father spoke to her when he first fell ill. *"God called us to make this journey . . . of that I am certain. I would lief die in this wild land of freedom than live in a land where worshiping God be a crime . . ."*

"Mary?"

"Sorry, Mother. I was woolgathering again."

"'Tis time for you to say farewell to your father." Mother's words choked in her throat, but Mary understood.

She stood up and leaned over, laying her face next to her father's. "Oh, Father . . . you brought us to this land of freedom, but—like Moses—you cannot cross over with us." She waited for the longest time, listening to his labored breathing. "No matter, Father, you are almost home." Somehow, when she said those last two words, she knew it for truth. "Aye, almost home."

※   ※   ※   ※

Three days later, Mary Allerton went into labor. Priscilla tended her at first, but when nothing progressed, Dr. Fuller took over. More than a day later she delivered, but her tiny boy was stillborn. Mary and Elizabeth kept Remember and her little sister, Mary, throughout the ordeal. Mistress Allerton asked to hold the wee babe until her husband returned. She sat rocking the tiny bundle, singing under her breath. "Hush a bye/ Do not cry/ Go to sleep-y, little baby/ When you wake/ You shall have/ All the pretty little horses."

Because they could not say how long the expedition would be gone, Elder Brewster gently took the little bundle for burial. Mary brought Remember and Little Mary to their mother and let them sleep close to help comfort her.

The explorers came home to a subdued company. When Elder Brewster took William Bradford aside to tell him of his wife's accident, the younger Bradford did not utter a word. From all the way across the darkened room, Mary saw the color drain from his face. He took his own blankets and went topside to sit at the place where his Dorothy most often waited for him. During the service that Elder Brewster gave in her memory, Master Bradford spoke not a word. As Mary brought him his soup, she could see the page marked "deaths" in his pocket notebook left open on the table. The page was blank except for the date and the words "Dorothy, Wife to Mr. William Bradford."

Father's death affected many. Being the oldest of the company, he was looked on as a father by several younger men. His committal service took place before the party returned.

Despite the losses, the Pilgrims needed to make a decision, so another meeting took place. The men intended to only recount the highlights but once they started the account, the passengers pressed for details.

"We sailed south, inside the bay," Governor Carver began. "The weather turned cold, and, at places along the shoreline, we broke ice to wade ashore." Several of the men made shivery gestures in agreement. "The sea spray whipped by the wind froze on our clothing till it felt like we were wearing coats of iron. Our teeth chattered so loudly, if Indians lurked nearby, they had ample warning of our approach.

"We stopped often to scout out possible sites along the route in case Plymouth would not be suitable. Captain Standish, please give account of our action at the place they call Nauset."

At the word "action" most of the younger boys looked up and scooted closer.

Captain Standish moved to the center, and, standing with military precision, he cleared his throat. "We sailed around a sandy point and put in at a bay. As we made for shore, we saw a group of Indians gathered around something massive, shiny, and black on the beach."

Some of the boys wriggled in anticipation.

"The Indians spotted us and became excited—hopping up and down and running in circles before they bolted for the woods." Captain Standish expanded on the story for the boys. "We built a barricade right there on the beach, using logs and stakes and pine branches. Built a blazing fire to give us warmth against the sleety, freezing wind."

"Did the Indians come?" Bartholomew knew better than to interrupt a meeting, but the story was so potent, he forgot the meeting for the storytelling.

Captain Standish, who loved to spin a good story, forgave the interruption. "Nay, they stayed away *that* night." He put the emphasis on "that." The suggestion made the boys poke each other with anticipation.

"The next morning we walked to the place where the Indians had been. The black thing was an immense fish—nearly fifteen feet long—like no whale or fish we had ever seen. 'Twas a funny thing . . ." He stopped as if to consider it all over again. "It had a layer of fat under the skin near two inches thick, like a hog."

He then told how they came upon a graveyard that looked much like a church graveyard with saplings set fencelike all the way around it.

Captain Standish explained that they moved the shallop a little further south and put up another barricade. "That night," he continued, "we were startled awake with a hideous cry. I yelled the call to arms, and we discharged our muskets into the pitch-black night, yet we heard nothing more. One of the sailors said the screams sounded like the wolves he once heard in Newfoundland, so all slept again except for the sentries.

"The next morning, we no sooner said prayers and sat down to a small meal, when we heard an unearthly scream much like the sound of the night before." Several of the men nodded their heads in agreement. "Some foolishly ran toward the shallop to retrieve their weapons." The captain's voice revealed his displeasure. "They came running into the barricade followed by a hail of arrows."

Governor Carver took out a bundle of arrows to show them. Some had eagle's claws as points, others had bits of sharpened deer horn. "The arrows flew all around us," he said. "They came so close we could hear the sound of the feathers whizzing past us in the air." He took his coat and put his fingers through a rip. "Arrows pierced many of the coats hanging in the barricade and yet not a one of us was wounded.

"My flintlock splintered a tree near one of the Indians and may have injured him, but we were fortunate in that no Indians were seriously injured before they ran away," Captain Standish said.

"This be good news," Elder Brewster said. "We continue to pray that we will be able to make a fair and long lasting treaty with the Indians when we settle."

The men took turns telling the rest—how they continued to sail around Cape Cod Bay until they hit a fearsome storm near the Plymouth Bay. It broke a rudder and split the mast as they furiously rowed away from thunderous breakers. The battered boat eventually landed at an island in the bay, which they promptly named Clark's Island for the ship's well-liked first mate. They spent the Sabbath there before rowing over to Plymouth on Monday.

The story up till now had been the groundwork. The young boys relished the Indian tales, but most of those gathered waited for the verdict. Had they found a home?

How Mary wished Father sat beside her. He had yearned for a land of freedom for as long as Mary could remember, and then he died when they were so close. 'Twas not fair. She saw Constance sitting near her father and Elizabeth standing beside hers. She knew they loved their families, but between them, they had brothers and sisters and aunts and uncles and cousins aboard. She looked at Mother, sitting with hands folded —Mother was all she had left.

Mary could little bear to hear the rest. If they settled in Plymouth, then so be it. She went to the *dower chest* and sat down. There among the bundles lay her gift from Isabella. *I should have opened it in Delft*, she thought. *Now, I no longer care.* She tossed it to the side—near the bundles, still packed, of her father's things. *Oh, Father . . . how shall I go on?*

"Mary?" Mother put her arm around Mary's shoulders.

"Mother, what shall we do?"

Mother sat down beside her on the chest without speaking. She seemed to know that the question required no answer.

"They still debate, Mary, but 'twould seem that Plymouth shall be our settlement at last." Mother gently ran the back of her fingers down the side of Mary's face. "We are almost home, little one."

Home.

Mary no longer even remembered what that meant. Perchance that word would forever remain a mystery to her.

10
The Mayflower
Nannies

S o, if we are finally home," Constance said, "why are we still living on this ship?"

"What we have here is . . . Constance complaining," Elizabeth said, laughing.

"I fear I may join her," said Mary. "I am hungry, I am sick of this ship, and I may never be warm again."

The *Mayflower* now lay anchored in the Plymouth harbor with the shallop bobbing alongside, waiting to take the first party to see their new home.

"I wonder who shall be chosen to go ashore at Plymouth first?" Elizabeth said.

"The 'who shall be first' debate may rage on until we are gray-haired grandmothers," Constance said with her ready laugh. "John Alden claims to have been the first Pilgrim to step foot on New England soil when he stepped out onto the shore at Cape Cod."

"One of the members of the third exploration party

would be first to step foot on Pilgrim soil. They came to Plymouth from Clark's Island."

"That shall not count," Elizabeth announced. "They were only exploring. We had not yet decided to settle in Plymouth." She continued her reasoning, "We only agreed to Plymouth after they returned to the *Mayflower* when she was still anchored at Cape Cod. So 'tis whomever steps first out of the shallop that earns the distinction." Elizabeth's serious face made both girls laugh.

The laugh surprised Mary. How good it felt to laugh. She would miss Father forever, but she knew—yes, she knew for certain that laughter rang throughout heaven. Maybe her happiness connected her more closely to her father, now, than sadness ever did.

It reminded her of something Mother said before they left Cape Cod. "'Tis far easier to embrace sadness than to reach for joy." Her mother spoke truth. *From now on, I shall work to take joy over sadness,* Mary decided, *as God is my strength.*

"Mary, your mother calls."

"And here I am woolgathering again. Thank you, Elizabeth." Mary went down to the cabin to find Mother.

"Mary, Governor Carver and Elder Brewster just spoke to me. They invited you to accompany the first party to see the new settlement."

"Me? Why?"

"In honor of your father. They knew how he longed for a land of freedom, so you shall see it in his place." Her mother squeezed her hand. "Put on your warmest things, Mary. Make haste so you don't miss the launch."

Mary ran to tell her friends, who squealed with happiness

for her. They both stood at the rail, waving and watching as the longboat pulled away from the ship.

The *Mayflower* anchored about a mile and a half from the shore, so 'twould not be an overly long trip. Mary's fellow passengers were mostly men, but some of the women went as well. The frigid wind whipped across the boat, and Mary's face and ears felt as if they might freeze. Her lips began to chap as well, so she wrapped her hood tighter. The water lapped against the boat in waves of choppy peaks, but it only added to the sense of adventure.

As the crew rowed into the harbor they headed for the huge granite rock that would allow passengers to step from the shallop without having to wade through water. As the men threw out the rope, Mary stood up and lightly stepped over the side onto the rock. *There.* Too bad Elizabeth and Constance were not along. They would have laughed till their sides hurt. Mary looked around. All the other passengers in the shallop busily gathered their things or tied the ropes or talked to each other—no one even noticed 'twas naught but a girl who stepped foot first.

The party made its way from the shore up a hill. Mary noticed fields already cleared and wondered who farmed here before. And where had they gone?

The men pointed out the fresh running water. As they came to the top of the hill, Mary wandered off by herself. When she looked back she saw a view that fair took her breath away. The beauty of the landscape—even this first day of winter—made her bend her knee and give thanks. Looking down the hill she caught the edge of the shore with the lapping water that stretched from Plymouth all the way to England and Holland.

She breathed deeply of the cold air until it filled her lungs. *This is what home smells like.* She reached down and scraped away the frozen ground until she could scratch a handful of Plymouth soil. Opening her pouch she took out her handkerchief with the Dutch soil and added this new handful.

She heard the shout that meant they were to go back to the shallop. Taking one last look around, she tucked the bulging hankie back into her pouch and ran down the hill until she caught up with the party.

Mary heard the reports each day along with the rest of the women. The bone-chilling work had begun on building shelter at Plymouth. No sooner would the men set up a plan than a storm would move in and gale winds would keep the shallop from carrying workers from their home on the *Mayflower* to the settlement at Plymouth.

The builders laid out the foundation for the Common House on the north bank of the brook. Small huts were constructed for the builders so that they could save the time of having to go back and forth from the ship to the settlement. Slowly, despite the foul weather, Plymouth began to take shape. Captain Standish built a platform for the cannon on the highest point where the fort would be built.

Life on the *Mayflower* became even more difficult. The unheated ship was damp and drafty, and the food stores dwindled. Everyone was hungry. Coughing fits could be heard all across the cabin, and many passengers sickened and kept to their beds.

"Mary, we will be moving over to Plymouth tomorrow. Our house is near finished." Constance spoke quietly. "I worry about leaving you and Elizabeth alone here—the work grows heavier each day with so many falling ill."

"We will be following soon enough. Since 'tis now just Mother and me, we will stay with the White family until a house can be built for us," Mary said. "But I will miss you, Constance."

Mary could not find words to say more. With Constance near, the girls always seemed able to summon up a laugh or find some way to lighten the load.

"Soon, we will all be together again."

Mary heard from some of the sailors that Constance and her family settled into their makeshift home in Plymouth. With the large Hopkins family gone as well as several other families, the days on the *Mayflower* moved even more slowly. Winter dragged on, one day looking much like the next. At least nighttime passed quickly, when Mary could burrow into her mattress and shut out the day's worries. The pitch black of the cabin, the gentle rocking of the boat, and the exhaustion of caring for so many sick ones helped ensure a sound sleep. Mary often dreamt of spring flowers and Holland.

"Mary?"

Mary nuzzled deeper into her covers. She dreamed that someone called her and shook her shoulder. She turned over,

trying to find a warm place on her feather tick. The movement of the boat bunched it up, and she was partially
scrunched under her mother's bunk. The thin blanket did little to keep the cold damp air off. Ever since they anchored in
Plymouth Bay she had taken to wearing layers of clothes to
bed—anything to try to keep warm.

"Mary?" Elizabeth whispered near her ear. "Are you
awake?"

"Elizabeth? Is something wrong?" Mary untangled her
legs and sat up, pulling her blanket around her.

Elizabeth sat down beside Mary, her blanket wrapped
around her shoulders. "Can we talk without waking your
mother?"

"I think so." Mother had never recovered energy since
Father died. At first Mary thought 'twas exhaustion, but then
the cough set in. Except for fits of coughing, Mary's mother
slept deeply. Waking her had become difficult even when she
thrashed about and slept fitfully.

"My mother has taken to her bunk." Elizabeth pronounced
those words in a whisper. "My aunt and uncle as well."

Mary understood the fear that brought her friend here.
"Oh, Elizabeth . . ." What could she say? That she understood that hollow feeling? That she, too, felt like a little lost
girl much of the time? None of those things needed to be put
into words. Her friend just needed to sit next to someone who
listened and understood.

"Father works to finish our house. He says the air on this
ship is unhealthy." Elizabeth paused, pulling the blanket
tighter against the chill. "In a *fortnight,* we shall all be in-

stalled in homes within the settlement, but . . . 'tis not just the ship. 'Tis more than that, Mary, I know it is."

Mary knew it as well. This winter had caught the small group unprepared. Because of all the delays, the New England winter had settled hard on them. Since just a few weeks out from England, they had braved ferocious winds, bone-chilling dampness, and bitter cold. Because of the political wrangling and manipulations by the colony's financial backers, food and supplies were in perilously short supply.

"How could God have brought us all this way only to let us die of cold and starvation?" Elizabeth asked the question that many pondered during sleepless nights.

"I wish I knew the answer to that question." Mary thought for a long time. "To know the answer would be to know the outcome of this pilgrimage. If it turns out to be successful, we will all look back—in those grandmother memories Constance is so fond of imagining—we will all look back and see God's hand in this despite the pain and the losses."

"'Tis true . . ."

"And if we all perish, what does that signify?" Mary sighed. "Remember the verse in the Scriptures that says 'to live is Christ, and to die is gain'?" I think that is how my father viewed death, but when you find yourself the one left behind, the dying part is a wrenching loss."

"I know. And we see such selflessness—like all the mothers who short their own rations to see that the children are fed." Elizabeth tucked her toes under the corner of Mary's blanket. "Now 'tis the mothers who seem to be the weakest."

Mary nodded her head. She knew. She watched her own mother grow weaker. "Are you well?"

"Hunger makes my head ache and my belly gnaw, but I remain strong. And you?"

"I, too, am well," Mary said. So far she remained strong, though she longed to be off the ship.

"Sometimes I feel as if everything I love—Father, my sisters, Fear and our other Green Gate friends, my home in England, my home in Leyden—everything slips away." Mary should have been comforting Elizabeth, but her own worries simmered close to the top.

"Except for leaving Holland, I have yet to suffer loss in my life," Elizabeth said. "I have no practice with hardship, Mary. What shall we do?"

"My mother always talks about 'casting cares on the Lord,'" Mary said. "'Tis easier talked about than put into practice, but I think practice is the key." Mary still struggled with this, but she tried to learn from her mother. More than once, when her mother ended a session of prayer, Mary watched a renewed look of peace settle on her face, and saw her mother wipe clean the wrinkled forehead and relax the clenched teeth of worry. Mother deliberately practiced handing over her troubles to God.

"Shall we help each other practice this, then?"

"We can surely try." Mary put her arm around her friend. "In the face of the hardship we ought to try to look for God's hand in bringing us to Plymouth. And keep reminding each other."

"Aye," Elizabeth said. "Perchance the reason we are still healthy is to help the others—that could be God's provision, could it not?"

"Indeed!" Mary knew Elizabeth was right and there was

much to do. "We need to begin preparations for our move ashore, helping pack those who are too sick."

"And we need to continue to gather the little ones together and care for them." The spark was back in Elizabeth's voice. "We talk about how deeply we feel the losses—think of these wee ones with mothers unable to care for them!"

"If we are to again become the *Mayflower* nannies, my friend, we had best get some sleep."

11

Samoset
and Squanto

Winter finally ended. Rough dwellings lined the dirt path from the top of the hill down toward the bay. The wave of sickness continued even after some of the Pilgrims moved into their unfinished homes in the Plymouth village.

At one point, only seven colonists were well enough to care for the others. Captain Standish and Elder Brewster were among them, tirelessly going from house to house bringing soup, airing bedding, and encouraging friends. The reports going back and forth between those on the *Mayflower* and those in the settlement were equally grave. By spring, more than half the Pilgrims and sailors had perished. Even the governor, Deacon Carver, died, so the colony appointed William Bradford to be their governor.

During the long trip from Leyden to America, Mary had used much of the idle time on the ship daydreaming about their eventual home. Her dream changed as the journey progressed, but the scene always played out on a sunny day with

Mother and Father and good friends nearby, a fire in the fire-place, and something bubbling on the hearth—maybe hodge-podge. Sometimes she pictured herself holding her long-ago gift from Isabella as she walked up the path to her new house. At the threshold of the house, she slowly unwrapped the package, remembering Holland and family and bringing them into her new life in America.

She had never pictured the months spent living aboard the *Mayflower* after landing or the heartbreaking sickness and death. She had never imagined the hunger always gnawing somewhere deep inside. She had never imagined that her father would not live to see their colony. A certain numbness had settled on Mary by the time her mother died. Toward the end, Mother had tried to prepare Mary.

Mother remained quiet as Mary fed her, aired the mattress on her bed, cleansed the sores on her legs, and helped her into a clean shift, but she seemed unusually alert. Mary wondered if she was recovering.

"Do you remember that weaving we talked about all those months ago?" Mother asked.

Mary did.

"And we talked about the cloth of our family being parceled out and even torn asunder." From the wistful look on Mother's face as she said this, Mary knew that she was thinking of Father's death—the worst rip of all.

"If you only remember one thing, Mary, remember that even when we cannot see the pattern in the fabric, or under-stand the purpose for which it is made, the Weaver still directs the whole undertaking."

"The weaver?"

"Aye. God is the one what weaves the cloth of our families." And no matter how sick Mother became, Mary could see that she believed it with her whole heart.

She died one night shortly afterward. That night, with the ship gently rocking, Mary had settled on the crate next to the bunk, holding Mother's hand. Mother had developed a deep rattle in her chest that seemed to get worse with each labored breath. It frightened Mary. Dr. Fuller sat with them for a time, but others needed him as well.

Mary meant to keep vigil all night long, but in the wee hours before dawn, she must have fallen asleep. When she awoke, her head rested on her arms at the edge of the bed. Her mother's arm lay across Mary's shoulders, but Mother had slipped away during the night.

Mary was alone.

All her life she had wanted nothing more than to belong, and now she found herself completely alone in a strange land. To the very end, her father held that God brought them on this journey. Her mother never wavered in her belief that God was still in control. Mary was mostly tired and didn't know what she thought.

When it came time to move into Plymouth, Mary's dreams no longer made sense. She was temporarily housed with Mistress White, who had lost her husband. Some of the sailors helped her move her things into the tiny house. Mary had them put the chest near the corner. She simply wedged the bundles between the chest and the corner. What sense was there in unpacking? The very last thing she threw on the pile was that stained oilcloth-covered bundle. Sitting there atop the other bundles it almost seemed to mock her. One day she picked up the gift and shoved it into the middle of the pile.

Spring finally arrived. With tree branches budding and the grasses on the hillside pushing through the soil, the small band of Pilgrims prayed that they had finally turned a corner. Only four women survived the winter—Constance's mother was one of those four. Elizabeth's mother was not.

The older girls—Priscilla and Desire along with the Carvers' maid, Dorothy—worked with the women to wash and cook and help get the crops planted. Mary, Elizabeth, and Constance continued to care for the five young children who lost their mothers. They helped with the other children as well.

Bartholomew Allerton was eight years old, so he spent much of his time with his father, but when he started missing his mother, Mary noticed he would come around and sit close when it came time to hear the stories. His sisters, Little Mary, who was four, and Remember, who was six, seemed as lost as Mary did most of the time. Their mother had never recovered from losing her stillborn son. She'd begun slowly slipping away that day.

Samuel Eaton had not yet reached his first birthday. His father survived, but not his mother. Constance spent most of her time caring for Samuel and her own infant brother, Oceanus, along with three-year-old Damaris.

Elizabeth's one-year-old cousin, Humility, was already an orphan when she had joined Elizabeth's family's voyage to America. Now she lost her aunt, who had become her new mother. She became Elizabeth's shadow. She cried if Elizabeth even left the room. At night Humility slept with her tiny hand curled around Elizabeth's finger. Sometimes Elizabeth also helped care for the youngest Pilgrim, Peregrine, since Mistress White and the other women had so much work to do.

One day the three girls gathered all their charges together in Elizabeth's house. The infants were napping. Humility slept without loosening her grip on Elizabeth's finger. Damaris napped as well.

"Do you think we'll ever see an Indian?" Bartholomew asked. He could barely sit still today, but Mary knew he needed to be "mothered" in their cozy circle, so she didn't insist that he go outdoors.

The colonists had observed Indians near the settlement in mid-February. Though the Indians still made no move toward contact, the colonists feared to let the Indians know of their weakened state. Even when the men were sick, they managed to prop themselves up against a tree with their muskets at the ready. They buried the dead under cover of night at the top of the hill in unmarked graves so any watching Indians would not observe the dwindling number of colonists.

"I do not know," Mary said honestly. "We hoped to make friends with them long before now."

"I want to make friends with an Indian," Remember said.

"Me, too," Little Mary agreed.

Six-year-old Resolved White had joined them this day as well. Because Mary lived in the White household, he claimed family rights to her. "Can we go out and find them, Mary? Can we?" He jumped up and down.

Constance gave an exasperated eyebrow signal to Mary, pointedly looking at the four tiny nappers.

"All right, Resolved. We shall go out and seek an Indian. Little Mary, Remember, and Bartholomew will help us."

Mary clapped a hand over Resolved's mouth before he let out one of his war whoops.

She bundled up her troop against the cool spring day and walked them up the hill toward the fort. The children reminded her of the goats she used to watch in Holland. They ambled along in a group until, all of a sudden, one would give a little leap for joy, and the happiness would ripple through the whole flock.

Mary saw the men outside the partially built palisade that would eventually encircle the entire village. They tilled the soil of the fields that were already cleared. They wanted to be ready to plant the baskets of seeds found at Corn Hill. She knew that they debated long and hard about how to plant these seeds—Indian corn was a new crop for them.

Mary remembered her promise to Elizabeth that they would remind each other about the provident acts of God on their behalf. In all the sorrow of winter, she had forgotten that promise. On this spring day, however, she thought about those seeds. *I shall remember to tell Elizabeth.* She looked down the hill and out to the water, thinking about how far they had come.

"Mary," yelled Bartholomew. "I see our Indian." The boy jumped up and down until his excitement had the other three hopping.

"Over there, Mary," Resolved said, pointing toward the field. Mary thought this was another one of their pretend games, until she turned in the direction Resolved pointed. There stood a tall Indian, talking to Captain Standish and the men. Mary watched as Governor Bradford gestured to the Indian to come inside the village. Captain Standish hung back and set up several men as sentries before joining the governor and the Indian.

"Mary," Elder Brewster called to her from across the field. "Will you ask Mistress Brewster to prepare a meal for our friend?"

"Aye, Elder Brewster," Mary said with a curtsey as she gathered the children and hurried over to the Brewster house.

She found Mistress Brewster already preparing dinner and relayed the message. Mistress Brewster gathered some biscuits and butter, some cheese and a pudding, along with a piece of roast duck. Tucking it into a basket, she handed it to Mary to take to the Hopkins house, where the men gathered. Mistress Brewster suggested she leave the children to play with Love and Wrestling.

When Mary walked into the house she didn't want to interrupt, so she walked to the lean-to portion and sat down with Constance.

"I've come to welcome you, Englishmen."

Mary and Constance exchanged surprised glances. This tall copper-colored man spoke the king's English. He also proudly wore a bright red wool horseman's coat. Mary knew he did not have it on when he walked into Plymouth—truth to tell, he wore very little clothing. The elder must have loaned him the coat out of modesty.

He told them his name was Samoset and he, too, was a foreigner from the land of "the people of the dawn"—the Wabenaki, from far away near Pemaquid. He learned to speak English from a fisherman who crossed the North Atlantic each year to fish for cod.

"Do you know who cleared the fields around here?"

asked Governor Bradford, motioning outside toward the fields. "And why they are not here?"

"Patuxet," Samoset said. "Name of people who live here." The man sat silent for a long time. "Four snows past—people all die. Great plague."

So that was why the fields were abandoned, and they had seen so few Indians. Mary's throat got tight. That story came too close to her own sadness. Some might say 'twas providence that caused the sickness so the Pilgrims could begin their colony on tilled soil without threat. Mary could never think that. She knew God loved those mothers and fathers and tiny babes just as surely as He loved her family. Perhaps God's providence merely led them to this abandoned site. She needed to remember to ask Elizabeth.

Samoset ate the meal prepared by Mistress Brewster and decided to spend the night in the village. Constance's father invited him to stay in their home. As Mary left to go back to her house, Constance fingered a lock of her hair and gave Mary a broad grin before she waved farewell.

Mary knew what she meant as well as if she spoke the words, "When I am a grizzled gray-haired grandmother, just think of the stories . . ." Mary laughed aloud as she made her way home. How she loved her friends.

"Father says that Samoset shall be our friend." Bartholomew stopped his play to make the statement.

Bartholomew, Resolved, Wrestling, and Love played Indian all morning long. Mary could see that they believed Samoset to be of mythic proportion. 'Twas true, he stood almost three heads higher than Captain Standish, but their beloved captain was teasingly called Captain Shrimp by many of the sailors.

"My father says that God sent Samoset to us," Love said.

Mary relished listening to the boys talk. After seeing Samoset over several days, she was inclined to agree. He brought five of his braves with him on the second visit, and the ladies fed them all.

"Here comes Samoset. He brings another friend," Resolved announced.

The Indian he brought was named Squanto. According to Samoset, Squanto was truly fluent in English, and the Pilgrims found this to be true.

That night at supper they all ate together, and Squanto told them his story. Mary's little band of children crowded in around him to hear.

"Ten summers ago, English traders came to these shores. When my people came to trade, several of us were captured and taken aboard ship to be sold into slavery in Spain."

Bartholomew interrupted. "How old were you?"

"Please excuse my son for interrupting," said Master Allerton with a pointed look at his son.

"Beg pardon," said Bartholomew as he hung his head.

"No. 'Tis a fair question, young brave," Squanto said. "I was older than you—perhaps nine summers."

"Once the ship landed, my people scattered, having been sold to all manner of folk. God was with me. I was sold to a gentle monk who taught me to love your God. I later traveled to England and went to work in the stables of a good man named John Slaney."

The story fascinated Mary as much as it did the children.

She looked over at her friends, and each was riveted by the telling. Mary knew that Constance collected the story for her gray-haired enjoyment. Elizabeth kept giving Mary meaningful glances. *Aye, my friend, I too see the hand of God's providence in this story.*

"John Slaney promised to buy my passage home—back to my people." Squanto paused. "When I finally returned to these shores, I had no people. All I found were bones bleaching in the sun. The sickness—I think similar to the smallpox I saw in England—wiped out the Patuxet."

Mary understood the emptiness in those words.

"All this time, I wondered why God brought me back to nothing." Squanto looked around the room. "Now I see."

Mary's heart thudded in her chest. Squanto asked the very question that haunted Mary. *Why did God bring me all this way for nothing?* Could Squanto have just shown her the answer? Remember and Little Mary came over and snuggled into Mary's lap. As Little Mary stuck her thumb in her mouth and fell asleep, Mary stroked her hair and drew the two little girls closer.

12
Giving Thanks

Squanto stayed. He believed God sent him to the Pilgrims. And, as Governor Bradford said of him on one Sabbath, "He became a special instrument sent of God for our good."

Squanto introduced them to Ousa Mequin, the Great Massasoit, chief of the powerful Wampanoag, who lived to the southwest on the Narragansett Bay. He helped them offer appropriate gifts, build a friendship, and negotiate a fair treaty.

Squanto also showed the Pilgrims how to fish and how to plant Indian corn. Mary knew that without his knowledge they likely would have starved.

"This cornfield is old ground," he told the planters. "You will have to fertilize each hillock with three herring."

"However will we catch that many fish?" asked Governor Bradford. They had little luck fishing.

"'Tis not been the proper time," Squanto said. "When the fish begin their run up the brook, 'twill be simple to set traps to catch them." He showed them how to make and set the traps, and the catch was more than sufficient to fertilize the field.

Once the field was planted, he instructed the men to guard the field all night long to keep the wolves from digging it up.

"What think you, Mary?" Elizabeth said one day. "It does not take much reminding to see the hand of the Lord on this endeavor anymore, does it?"

"Nay," Mary said with conviction. "My heart burned, and anger began to kindle against God, but watching His care of us—whether it is through a miracle like Squanto or the simple everyday provisions—there be no denying His hand, Elizabeth." Mary knew her father was right when he insisted that this was God's will for them, even though her father could not cross over with them into Plymouth. "Thank you, Elizabeth, for helping me learn to look for God's hand in our journey."

Mary's mother had insisted that the Weaver always directed the entire undertaking—now Mary could begin to see the pattern, and she knew her mother had the right of it.

When the time came for the *Mayflower* to make the trip back across the Atlantic, Captain Jones asked each person if they wanted to return to the safety of England. Mary thought of her family—Isabella, Ingle, and Christian—back in Holland. She still missed them. But as she looked 'round the room at the faces here—Constance, Elizabeth, Elder Brewster, Squanto, and her little band of children—she knew. Nay, she would not join Captain Jones; she would stay in Plymouth.

Not a single Pilgrim boarded the ship to sail back to England.

New life sprang up all around them. Now that the crops

were in, the first wedding of the colonies would take place. Edward Winslow, who lost his wife in the sickness, and Susannah White, who lost her husband, announced that they planned to be married.

The trip to Corn Hill to return the borrowed seed took place soon after harvest. Everyone continued to work hard. Before long eleven houses lined the street. Each house had a good-sized garden space plotted out. Mary often sat with her children to dig in the warm loamy soil with clamshell scoops.

"Mary?" Remember sat in the garden with Mary. "Is this dirt so very different from the dirt in Leyden?"

"I cannot say, Remember." How could Mary have forgotten her pouch of soil she carried all the way from Delft? "Next time we come to dig in the garden, I will bring soil from Holland and we will see."

Harvest was plentiful, and they were able to add to the daily food ration for each family. When everything had been gathered together, the company looked over their blessings and decreed a celebration "after a more special manner," the governor said, "to rejoice together."

The children bubbled with excitement. "We will have a time of thanksgiving, Mary," Bartholomew said as Mary and the children played near the springhouse. "We will eat and play games and—"

"We shall pray as well, Bartholomew." Remember liked to correct her older brother.

"My mother and Priscilla and Dorothy and Desire have been cooking and cooking and cooking. Only other thing they been doing is making us stay out of the house," Resolved complained.

"That's because 'twill be such a feast, and 'tis likely to go on for days," Mary said. "The Great Massasoit brings ninety guests with him. Did you see them leave to hunt deer to bring to the feast?"

Elizabeth walked over with Humility. "Do you know what we shall be eating?" She shook her head in wonder. "I just took Peregrine home and saw what they are preparing. Besides the venison, we shall have roast duck, roast goose, clams, fish, succulent eels, white bread, corn bread, leeks, watercress and other salad herbs, and dried berries. Can you believe it, Mary?"

"'N' plums," Humility added.

"That is true, wee girl, wild plums as well." Elizabeth gave the tiny girl a kiss.

"Shall we scrub faces, wash hands, and go over to help spread the tables for the first meal, Mary?" Elizabeth asked.

"Scrub faces?" shrieked Bartholomew. "That will ruin the day for a certainty!"

"Elizabeth, can you take the children? I'd like to go home and get one of Mother's tablecloths from the *dower chest*. 'Twould almost be like having Mother present at the feast. I shall be there presently."

She ran home after washing her own face and hands. Opening the chest, she took out Mother's linen tablecloth, smoothing her hands over the texture of the weaving. *Aye, Mother, I have made a beginning to understand about the Weaver. Not everything, but some of it.*

She looked at the bundles, still crammed in beside the chest. *Heavenly Father, 'tis time. 'Tis time to thank You for Your provision. 'Tis time to acknowledge that You directed my path all the way home. That gnawing, aching longing for home—for a place to belong—that longing is gone. I still miss Mother and Father. I think I always shall.* Mary dropped to her knee right there by the chest. *Perhaps it matters not where I am, but that my home is in You. Father, I thank Thee. Amen.*

As she leaned forward on the chest to push herself up, she saw the oilcloth bundle tucked into the pile. How could she have forgotten Isabella's gift? She tied her pouch around her waist, put the tablecloth over her arm, and took Isabella's gift.

The first meal of the harvest feast passed almost too quickly. The plentiful food, the table filled with friends both old and new, the children running, and the prayers of thanksgiving—it was all too good to be over so soon. Mary was glad this was only the first day of many.

Constance, carrying a sleeping Samuel, said, "This shall be one of those unforgettable memories, will it not?"

"Indeed," whispered Mary, afraid to wake the sleeping infant. "Can you come with me? I need to find Elizabeth."

They found Elizabeth and gathered their children.

"Mary wants to show us something!" said Little Mary.

"This is a gift my sister gave to me more than a year ago in Holland. I decided then to wait to open it until I was finally home." Mary's throat felt tight. "All this time I thought home was a place, but this afternoon I understand that God had indeed guided me home—home to Him, though it took me most of my life to realize it."

"Open it, Mary," Bartholomew said excitedly. "We want to see your present."

Mary slowly untied the knots, remembering the terrible storm that they had weathered along the way. She took the oilcloth off and gave it to Constance. "Keep this to remind you of the storm we weathered." Mary laughed. "'Twill be a grandmother memory."

She unwrapped the linen wrapping and when she saw the contents, her eyes filled with tears. Isabella could not have given her a gift more *dear.*

"'Tis nothing but some old shriveled onions," Resolved said with scorn and disappointment in his voice.

"Nay, my little friend, 'tis much more than that. Come with me." Mary led the group over to the garden plot. Their clamshells were still poked in their most recent diggings.

Mary dug three holes in the raised bed. She opened her leather pouch and took out the hankie filled with soil. "Remember asked me if our Plymouth dirt was any different from our Holland soil. In all the sorrowing of the winter I forgot about these handfuls of dirt." Mary untied the hankie. "This is dirt from Holland mixed with soil from up by the fort." She put some of the soil into each of the holes she had made in the ground.

She took the "onions" out of the linen. "And these are lily bulbs. Come spring, the Madonna lilies that sprout will fair take your breath away."

"Lilies? Oh, Mary." Elizabeth knew how much flowers meant to Mary.

"Isabella remembered." Mary had to stop for a minute. "Long ago, in Leyden, I prayed that I would one day have a garden with plenty of room in which to tuck flowers. I told the Lord that then I would know I was home." Mary spread her arms wide. "Cramped into a tiny house in Leyden 'twas naught but a dream, but look! Look what we have spread before us."

Mary gave the linen scrap to Elizabeth. "Keep this piece of linen, Elizabeth. It came from Leyden. You were right about God's providence." She folded the piece and gave it to her friend with a smile. "I shall tell you later about the Weaver."

She put the bulbs into the ground and firmed the soil over the top. "In the sadness I forgot all about beauty and flowers. And all this time this gift sat among my bundles, waiting to remind me that I was almost home."

Epilogue

The story of the Pilgrims' journey to America is the story of God's providence. Mary Chilton, Constance Hopkins, and Elizabeth Tilley were all actual passengers on the *Mayflower*. While we don't have a record of what they actually said to each other, all the events in the book are true—right down to Francis Billington nearly blowing up the *Mayflower*.

Up until recent years, Mary Chilton's family was always listed with the Strangers—those who were not part of the *Separatist* movement. Thanks to recent researchers, records were found to prove that they were, indeed, Saints. The rock-throwing incident in Leyden really happened—the magistrate's record of it helped place the Chiltons in Leyden. Another important discovery was the *excommunication* of Mary's mother in Sandwich.

The treaty that Squanto helped forge between Massasoit and the Plymouth Colony lasted for decades, and the Pilgrims and the Native Americans lived together in peace and friendship.

Mary's friend Fear Brewster stepped off the *Anne* in Plymouth Harbor in 1623. Mary's sister Isabella and her family eventually came to America as well. The colony blended in a number of ways over the years. Mary grew up to marry John Winslow, who came to the colony on the *Fortune,* arriving just a few weeks after that first Thanksgiving. He was the brother of Edward Winslow, so Susannah White Winslow became Mary's sister-in-law. Mary and John eventually had ten children of their own.

The "General Sickness" that took so many lives that first winter is thought to have been a combination of *scurvy*—a disease caused by the lack of vitamin C—and pneumonia. All the children who were orphaned that winter were welcomed into other families. Mary probably lived with the Standish or Alden families until she moved into the Winslow family when she eventually married.

The reason the study of the Pilgrims in America still intrigues us all these years later is that, as Americans, it is our story—a story of courage, faith, and perseverance against all odds.

Glossary

Apothecary chest. A place where medicines were kept.

Barbaric. Cruel and primitive.

Bard. Singer-storyteller.

Bark-rigged. Rigged with three or more masts.

Baste; basting. To make long running stitches in fabric. Used to temporarily hold fabric together while permanent stitching is applied.

Belaying pin. A post on the deck of a ship used for tying sails and other things down.

Boathook. A pole with a hook on the end.

Bosun. The shortened word for boatswain, the person in charge of rigging and anchors, among other things, on a ship.

Brackish. Salty.

Brazier. A small coal or wood stove used for cooking, similar to modern grills.

Breeches. Short baggy pants that fastened under the knee.

Brocade. A type of fabric.

Cached. Stored in a hidden location for future use.

Chamber pot. A pot kept near the bed for nighttime bathroom use.

Coif. A head covering for girls and women made of white linen that covered the hair.

Confinement. The time of childbirth.

Cooper. Barrel maker.

Corselet. Hammered metal armor used to protect the body from arrows.

Dear. In this context, it meant that something was special, rare, or expensive and difficult to replace.

Dissenter. A person who did not agree with and follow the rules of the official Church of England.

Doublet. A jacket worn over a shirt that was sometimes padded or quilted.

Dower chest. A wooden chest in which girls would collect items that they would use for their own home once they were married. After marriage, the dower chest would be used for storage.

Dray. Wagon.

Excommunication. Banished from the official church, in this case, the Church of England.

Fortnight. Two weeks.

Halyard. A rope that is rigged to raise a sail.

Heel; heeled. Tip or lean.

Interfacing. An interlining between the lining and the outer fabric that shapes the garment.

Jurisdiction. The area that government authorities are in charge of and have control over.

Klompen. The Dutch word for wooden shoes.

Leading strings. Strips of fabric sewn to the child's clothing at the shoulders that were used to help children learn to walk. Also used to control children's movements.

Lief. Rather.

List. Tip or lean.

Magistrate. A government official.

Mevrow. The Dutch title for married women.

Mewling. Crying like a baby.

Mind. In this case, obey.

Minding. In this case, baby-sitting.

Mizzenmast. The third mast on a ship.

Mynheer. The Dutch title for men.

Nappies. Diapers.

Nicked. Stole.

Patent. An official document that gave permission to settle on certain land.

Pin poppet. A cloth organizer for straight pins.

Poppet. A term of endearment for children, in this case used for dolls.

Privy. An outhouse.

Quay. Wharf.

Ruffs. Large fancy ruffled fabric or lace worn around the neck.

Scurvy. An illness caused by the lack of vitamin C.

Separatists. Those wanting to remain separate from the Church of England because of theological disagreements.

Sticking plaster. A powder, when mixed with water, which made a plaster that was used to close wounds.

Sweetbag. A bag in which sewing supplies were kept.

Topsail. An upper sail.

Trencher. A flat piece of wood used as a plate.

Courage to Run

Born Arminta Ross, young Harriet Tubman (named after her mother when she was full-grown) was a faithful strong girl growing up in the late 1800's as a slave in the south. The story of her childhood is a record of courage and bravery. Even more, it's the story of God's faithfulness as He prepares her to eventually lead more than 300 people out of slavery through the Underground Railroad.

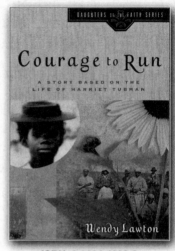

ISBN: 0-8024-4098-3

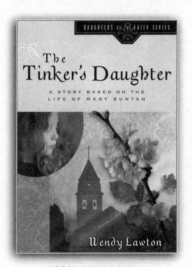

ISBN: 0-8024-4099-1

The Tinker's Daughter

John Bunyan, the author of *Pilgrim's Progress*, mentions only one of his six children in his memoirs—Mary. Born blind in 1650, her story still intrigues us nearly 350 years later. When her father was imprisoned for unlawful preaching, it was 10-year old Mary who traveled the streets of Bedford each day, bringing soup to her father in prison.

MOODY
PUBLISHERS
THE NAME YOU CAN TRUST.